# HIS HUNTER

## IVY MARIE

IVY MARIE PUBLISHING

# CONTENTS

# PROLOGUE

## ALICE

"VERY GOOD ALICE." DADDY beamed with pride. "That's enough for tonight."

I lowered the wooden sword I was using to my side, taking a moment to catch my breath before looking up at him with a pleased smile. I took to the sword effortlessly. Walking over to a table, I returned the wooden sword. I looked at the other weapons that filled the table wistfully — one day. Hopefully soon, I'll be able to train with those items too.

"Daddy, why does mommy not like the word Hunter?"

"Your mother doesn't approve of the Hunter lifestyle."

"Why?" I frowned, looking back up at him. "You said Hunters protect."

"Hunter is just a name." He explained, kneeling to be at eye level with me. "It was given to the brave men who picked up a weapon and fought against the supernatural. A very, very long time ago, the supernatural terrorized humans. Being a Hunter was very dangerous back then. They didn't have the skills, knowledge, or weapons we have today. You must remember, Alice, the relationship between Hunters and the supernatural was different when Hunters first emerged. Back then, it was kill or be killed."

"Is mommy still afraid of them?"

He took hold of my hands. "She is very afraid. She is even more afraid of you going after them and getting hurt."

"Mommy doesn't need to be scared." I told him confidently. "You said there is peace now."

"Peace never lasts long." He kissed my forehead before standing back up. "Go clean up. I'm taking you and your mother out tonight."

I hugged Daddy. I was excited to see where he was going to take us. I ran up the two levels of spiralling stone stairs to Daddy's study. Once upstairs, I slowly opened the door leading to the hallway, looking in both directions. No one was around. I slipped out of the study, turning to close the door very quietly.

"Alice Marigold Thorpe!" An all too familiar accusing tome came from behind me.

"Eep!" A startled sound escaped me.

"What do you think you're doing?"

"I, uh, was looking for Daddy."

I turned around very slowly to face Mommy with a sheepish grin. If she knew what I was doing, it would only scare her, and I don't want her scared. She stared down at me disapprovingly, her arms crossed. She must know I lied. She always seems to know when I lie. Her eyes narrowed as she took in my attire.

"Go shower. You look like you've been rolling around in the dirt."

"Yes, Mommy."

I scurried past her. After the much-needed shower, I found a dress on my bed. Mommy would have set it out for me while I was in the

2

bathroom. I dressed and then sat at the vanity set in my bedroom to brush out my long hair.

"Here." Mommy entered the room. Taking the brush from my hands, she began smoothing out the strands. "You need to be on your best behaviour tonight. There will be many important people will be at this dinner."

"Of course."

She styled my hair in a simple half-up crown braid. "There. You look so pretty."

"Not as pretty as you."

"Thank you." She smiled, kissing the top of my head. "Let's go. Your father is waiting for us."

Daddy stood at the bottom of the stairs. His smile was bright and loving as he looked up at us. We met him at the bottom, where he pulled Mommy in for a kiss before leading us out the front door. A car was already pulled out of the garage and waiting for us. I slid into the back seat, my parents occupying the front. Daddy drove down the driveway, onto the street, and out of our gated neighbourhood.

I gawked as Daddy pulled up to our dinner destination — a large royal-looking residence with a wide welcoming staircase and gold adorning the outside. A valet took the keys from Daddy. We followed other guests into the house. The inside of the house was just as grand as the outside. Staring up at the sparkling chandelier, I fell behind as my parents continued into the house.

"Alice?" Daddy called.

"Coming."

I rushed to rejoin my parents. Daddy waited for me at the door to the parlour. The many guests mingled in the large room. I stayed quiet as my parents mingled with the guests. Eventually, Mommy wandered off to chat with other women at the event. I slipped my hand into Daddy's, wanting to stay with him.

"Hunter." A wonderfully musical voice spoke from behind us.

"Queen." Daddy turned from the gentleman he was speaking with.

"Who is this?" She questioned.

Her bright green eyes rested on me. Distracted by her beauty, I almost forgot my manners. The woman was stunning in her sleek black dress. Taking hold of the skirt of my dress, I curtsied just like Mommy taught me.

"Alice Thorpe." I told her.

"My daughter. She will replace me in due time."

"Ah." Understanding flickered on the woman's features before a serene smile graced her lips. "It's a pleasure to meet you, young Hunter."

"This is Queen Ana." Daddy explained. "She reigns over all the vampires in Stellacote and the surrounding cities. She's also in charge of the Sanguis in the country. Tonight, Queen has graciously opened her doors for us."

"A pleasure to meet you Queen Ana." I curtsied again. "You have a very pretty home."

"Let me introduce you to Joel and Josie Walker." Queen gestured to two similar-looking brown-haired children who came to stand on either side of her. "They will be your daytime contacts, young Hunter."

The chiming of a bell announced dinner. I joined a separate table with the other children. Josie and I became fast friends. Joel, on the other hand, scowled at me the entire time. I tried to befriend him but couldn't get him to remove that scowl. However, Josie's bright personality more than made up for his sourness.

After dinner, Daddy guided me to a room in the back of the house. This room contained one large table with many chairs. The chairs around it slowly filled with men from tonight's dinner and their sons. At least, I think it's their sons. The boys appeared to be around the ages of six to thirteen.

Once every male was seated, Daddy stood to speak. "Thank you, fellow Hunters, for coming. I know it has been a long trip for many of you. At this meeting, I officially want to introduce my daughter, Alice, as the next Hunter in the Thorpe line."

Murmuring erupted around the table. I offered a tentative wave from my seat next to Daddy. Being the only female in this male-dominated room, I felt small and insignificant. From further down the table, a red-headed boy waved back. That single gesture offered me a little confidence to smile at the group. Subtle nods, small smiles, and soft clapping soon greeted me from the other Hunters.

Suddenly the doors to the room swung open with such force that they banged against the walls. All eyes were on the figure standing in the doorway.

"What's all this?" The figure demanded. "The Hunter Society altogether, and no one invited me?"

I sunk back in my chair. Something about this man sent a sliver of fear up my spine. The tiny amount of confidence I'd gained vanished in an instant. The man's eyes swept over the room. There was something primal and dangerous in his gaze.

"Alex Kingsley." Daddy took point answering him. "You have been removed from the Hunter Society."

"And why is that?" The man glared.

"You do not follow the Hunter guidelines." Daddy stated bluntly. "Therefore, you do not have what it takes to be a Hunter."

"I don't have what it takes?" The man let out a harsh laugh. He strolled deeper into the room. "I handle the supernatural, something none of you seem to appreciate. You've all gone soft. Having dinner in the home of the vampires, letting wolves run around with humans. You have no pride as a Hunter."

"You are harming the peace." Someone said.

"The balance needs to be maintained." Another person continued.

"Alex." Daddy spoke with an air of authority in his tone. "Leave now while you still have dignity in your name."

The man scowled, looking around the room again, meeting the eyes of every Hunter around the table. "You will all regret this decision."

His pale green eyes fell on me. A slow smile curved his lips. I shivered. Daddy threw an arm out, blocking his view of me. Two Hunters stood suddenly. They each took hold of the man's arms and roughly escorted him out of the room. Daddy sat back down in the chair heavily. I don't understand anything that just happened. Still, I reached out to take Daddy's hand in mine. He smiled softly, pulling me closer to kiss the top of my head.

# Chapter One

## Ryan

This is the third time in the past two weeks that my partner, Detective Bret Michaelson, and I have been called to Capital Hill. A gated community housing the most influential families in Stellacote. Because of this, we've been pressured by Captain Hugh Forest and the mayor to catch the killer.

An officer on the scene greeted us at the front door. He briefly summarized what we're about to walk into: three victims, each found in separate rooms, with no evidence thus far of the killer. Same M.O. as the past two crime scenes we're still trying to solve. With nonverbal communication, Bret and I split up. He went to view the crime scenes while I went to speak with the house owners.

The sounds of sobbing guided me to a luxurious front parlour. I recognized the elderly man sitting bone straight on the couch as Judge Colt, his arm around his wife. She leaned into him, her face stained with tears. A middle-aged man sat on the other side of her. I assumed it was their son. A glance at family pictures framed on a few pieces of furniture confirmed my suspicion. The son's hands clenched in his lap as a junior detective — Baxter Jones — took their statements.

"Evening." I interrupted, maintaining an apologetic tone. "My name is Detective Ryan Lune."

"Curtis Colt." The judge acknowledged with a curt nod.

"Could you please recant the evening events until the victims were discovered?"

"We've already told him." The son jerked his chin to Baxter.

"And I appreciate that. We will have a written report of the events on file. I would like to hear the events for myself."

"Very well detective." Judge Colt replied coolly. His stern expression was unfamiliar to me outside of a courtroom. "We were out at the opera house earlier today. There was a matinee showing of *La Cenerentola*. Then we came home and had supper. My wife and I then made our way upstairs shortly after for bed. We have an early flight out tomorrow."

I nodded. Very little detail, but straight to the point. Protocol dictates that I should tell them not to leave town in case I need to contact them again. Though, leaving town might be safer for the Colt family. Besides, I don't believe they are the killers in tonight's crime.

"What time did you come home?" I prompted for more information.

"About four, maybe four-thirty."

I turned to their son. "What did you do after supper?"

"I went to the study." The son's tone was irritable. "I had two brandies when I thought I heard a sound. Going to investigate, I found the body in the kitchen."

"What time was this?"

"Around six." His brows knitted together as he thought about it. "Yes. I remember glancing at my watch when the butler came in to see if I needed anything else. That's when I heard the sound. I had him clean up the brandy glass while I went to investigate. After finding the body in the kitchen, I called the police and checked on my parents."

"What was the sound you heard?"

"A thud, like something heavy was dropped."

"Were there any signs of someone else in the house?"

"No."

"Detective." Mrs. Colt sniffled, trying to regain her composure. "Find the villain who did this."

"We will do our best." I pulled a business card from my wallet, handing it over for any of them to take. "If you can think of anything else, no matter how insignificant it may seem, call me."

The son tentatively took the card. I don't expect to hear from them, but offering never hurts. The families in Capital Hill tend to keep their private lives very private. I left the Colts in their parlour. With Baxter following me, we went in search of Bret. We found him in the study, kneeling over a male body. It appeared to be the butler. The overpowering scent of a slowly rotting corpse hit me hard in the sealed-off room. I scowled, wishing there was a window that could be open.

"Anything?"

"Nothing new here." Bret looked up at me from over his glasses. "Jugular has been ripped out just like all the other victims."

I turned to Baxter. "Have the coroner get the bodies ready. Maybe he can find more when he gets them on a table."

The young man nodded, leaving my partner and me alone with this body. I watched him go, ensuring we were alone, before returning my attention to Bret.

"What else?"

"The unknown vampire's scent is strong. Lingering on the bodies and in the room but nowhere else in the house. Except, of course, the other two crime scenes."

"Which collaborates the Colt family's testimony of finding the bodies today and immediately calling the cops." I ran a hand down my face. "I'll try contacting Queen again. There is no way she knows nothing about these murders or the killer."

Bret stood as the coroner entered the room. "She shut you down in record speed last time. So, what makes you think she'll talk to you this time?"

"I won't take no for an answer." I let out a low growl of annoyance.

"Then it's best we confront her now." Bret suggested. "Before she has time to learn about these murders and devise another excuse to turn you away."

Making our way out of the house and to the car, I paused with a hand on the door. "Who were the other victims?"

"A young maid was found in the bathroom; she appeared to be cleaning the toilet when attacked. The chef was the other victim, found lying on the kitchen island sprawled out like a meal."

I cringed at the description. Then, yanking the car door open, I slid inside and started the vehicle. Bret slid into the passenger seat and closed the door more gently than I did.

"A butcher knife was in the wall as if she threw it at her attacker." He continued. "I had forensics bag it and test it to see if she nicked him."

"I doubt it, but worth a shot. That must have been the sound the son heard, which left the butler alone in the study."

"When are you going to tell the Hunter?" Bret questioned casually as he buckled himself in.

"I won't be."

"Captain Forest won't be able to keep this one out of the media. She will find out, and when she does, she won't be happy with you."

"I can handle her." I ground out.

Bret's lips twitched. "I'm sure you can."

I frowned at my partner. The comment is far too knowing and far too amused for my liking. Placing the car in drive, I began leaving the Colt driveway when my phone, connected to the car's Bluetooth, began to ring.

"Detective Lune."

"Ryan." The Hunter's panic-stricken voice echoed around us.

"Alice?"

I hit the brakes waiting for her to answer. Silence on the other end had me panicked.

"Murder. My house. Va-ahh!" Her words cut off with a scream.

"Alice?" My heart pounded wildly in my chest. "Alice!"

There was no answer. The line had cut abruptly. I didn't think, only reacted. If Alice is in trouble, I need to be there. I hit the gas pedal and floored it out of the Colt driveway. Bret held onto the safety bar as I took corners fast, driving deeper into Capital Hill to the Thorpe residence.

I'd met Alice roughly five years ago when I was tracking down a newly changed wolf who was abusing women. I found the wolf at her feet with a silver dagger buried deep in his chest. She claimed it was self-defence, and I didn't think twice about it then. But, I'll admit, I was distracted by how beautiful I found her and by the scent of candy apples that seemed to wrap around her like the world's most enticing perfume. Her scent stirred my wolf into a frenzy that I struggled to keep at bay.

I thought it was a coincidence that I'd smelt her sweet scent at another crime scene just a few months later. Then I became suspicious when she seemed involved or at least nearby with every supernatural crime scene I encountered in the following couple of years. Eventually, I tracked her down and confronted her in her apartment. Our identities as Alpha and Hunter were exposed during a heated conversation, leading to an unexpected passionate kiss. My wolf urged me to claim her in that heated moment.

I knew I couldn't have her, didn't deserve her, but it didn't stop me from being protective and possessive of the Hunter with every rare meeting. She usually met me at her apartment whenever I itched to see her again, while she came to the station occasionally. I'd use the pretext of wanting her help with a case involving the supernatural as my excuse to see her again. She became a drug I never want to give up, a harsh reminder of what I can never have.

I could smell her interest with each visit, adding to her intoxicating sweet scent. It's a battle to keep my wolf in check whenever she's nearby. She keeps me at bay by using our status in the city as an excuse. Part of me wants to throw her reasoning out the window, but another part is glad for her justification. A monster like me doesn't deserve to be happy or loved. She deserves someone better than me.

The Thorpe driveway was lined with various cars, and lights were on in almost every room. There must be a party going on. Parking as close to the door as possible, Bret and I jumped out. Partway up the steps to the front door, a scream pierced through the night. I continued to the house as Bret shifted directions and headed to the back, where the scream came from.

I took a brief moment to register a small crowd of people at the end of the hall. Their nervous chatter was muffled by my heart pounding in my ears. Underneath their varying scents laid the scent of that vampire. It isn't normal to be able to smell the vampire outside of one particular room. My muscles tensed, and the fear of Alice being a victim forced me to focus on the scents. My nose led me upstairs. I burst into a room where I found Alice in the arms of some dark-haired male. I wanted to rip them apart and hold her close.

"Ryan." She whispered, relief evident on her face.

"Miss Thorpe." I stood my ground, reminding myself of our current location and her constant reminder of our social standings. "Are you okay?"

# CHAPTER TWO

## ALICE

I SAT STILL AS the make-up artist and hair stylist worked. My butt was killing me, and my legs were going numb. Finally finished, they took a step back, admiring their work before leaving me alone in my bedroom. Standing from the chair they'd set me in, I moved to the full-length mirror to examine the whole ensemble. I scowled at my reflection. Though the make-up and hair were simple, elegant, and very pretty, I didn't recognize myself. The form-fitting floor-length maroon dress made me feel restricted and uncomfortable. I itched to wash the make-up off and to strip into jeans and a T-shirt.

"You look stunning." My mother complimented, coming into view behind me, a pleased expression reflecting in the mirror.

"Maybe." I partially agreed. "But this isn't me."

Ignoring my discomfort, she continued. "You are bound to find a fiancée tonight. No man in their right mind wouldn't give you a double take."

"Mother, this isn't right."

"Nonsense. It was at one of these social gatherings that I met your father. We were married within the year. With the number of young

14

bachelors coming here tonight, I do not doubt that you'll find some one that gets your heart racing."

I bit the inside of my cheek. Of course, if she knew someone outside what she'd call 'our social circle' has already captured my heart, she would freak out. But I swear, my mother already has a vision of what my perfect match would look like.

"What if that doesn't happen? What if I don't find that person among the guests you've invited?"

"You can't stay twenty-eight forever." Her gaze sharpened on me through the mirror. "I do not doubt that you will find someone tonight. That young man will have the honour of protecting you from the dangers that lurk in this world."

"Mother." I let out an exasperated sound.

"Put some jewellery on and come downstairs." The older woman spun on her heels. "Our guests should be arriving shortly."

Five years ago, I tried moving out. I got an apartment and finally felt free. Barely a month later, my mother dragged me back to Capital Hill. Well, sort of dragged. She'd heard about women being attacked by an unknown assailant and insisted I return home. Little did she know I dealt with that assailant. I'd vehemently refused to return to this house until my father explained the situation.

It took only a day for my mother to break down. He took her to see doctors and therapists. They'd tentatively diagnosed her with separation anxiety disorder. The disorder is commonly seen in children who do not want to be away from their parents, and my mother was showing similar symptoms. However, the doctors and therapists said she could also have an adjustment disorder characterized by symptoms

15

such as anxiety. It was challenging to determine for sure. Either diagnosis was terrible.

I moved back home for my mother's mental health, and I've felt stuck in a gilded cage while walking on eggshells.

For my sanity, I would sneak out when my mother was asleep at night to fulfill my duties as a Hunter. And to get that freedom I so desperately crave. It has only been the last couple of years since my mother showed signs of healing when I carefully broached the subject of wanting to move out again. Which is how this match-making party came to be. The only way to leave this house is with a fiancée.

I grabbed a pair of floral ear cuffs and a matching necklace from the drawer of the vanity set. I paused in front of its mirror to plaster a smile on my face. My mother looked up and smiled approvingly at me when I came down the stairs. I stood by the front door with my parents, greeting everyone who came in: husbands, wives, sons, and a few daughters. I felt like an art piece the way I was quickly scrutinized as each guest entered.

The guests were directed into the parlour room, where drinks and hors d'oeuvres were served on silver platters. After the last guest entered, I followed my parents to the parlour room. I went around the room, politely playing the perfect daughter for my mother as she introduced me to each potential fiancée and his family.

Once the tour of the room was complete, I was free game. Each fiancée prospective swarmed me, asking questions and trying to boost themselves. Unfortunately, all I saw were weak, pampered boys. None of them fit to become a Thorpe and become a Hunter. Scratch that. I don't want my future husband to take that title from me. These boys aren't even fit to help care for any wounds inflicted on me. They'd probably pale and faint at the sight of a bit of blood.

"Please excuse me."

I could hold the forced smile briefly and was just about at my limit. I needed to step away, not wanting my mother to scold me if she saw me frowning. I pushed through the group of too-eager males surrounding me. This party is too suffocating. I need to find a way to escape. I slipped into the parlour's adjoining room — the sunroom. I could see the sun setting through the windows as I rubbed my jaw.

"Overwhelming, isn't it?"

Startled, I spun to see a good-looking dark-haired male and forced myself to smile. "What is?"

He frowned. "The attention, the fake smile."

I let the smile fall. "How did you know?"

"I have the same one." His lips quirked upward. "The smile that can fool a parent who isn't truly seeing you."

"Mother or father?"

"Father."

"Mother for me." An honest smile curved my lips. I extended my hand. "Alice."

"Lucas." He took my hand, kissing the back of it. "It is a pleasure to meet you."

"What brings you here?"

I took my hand back, resisting the urge to wipe it on my dress. His touch put me on edge. He didn't do anything to warrant the reaction, but my gut tightened in warning. I took a subtle step back.

"You." He stated flatly, then chuckled. "It is rather difficult to speak to a beautiful woman when surrounded by other men wanting her attention."

"What would you have said if other men didn't surround me?"

"I'd tell you how your beauty enraptured me the first moment I saw you."

I frowned, quirking a brow. "My beauty enraptured you?"

Lucas grinned. "I didn't think you'd go for that line. Can't blame me for trying."

"No, I wouldn't fall for that line. It might be among the top ten cheesiest lines I've heard all night." I crossed my arms.

He put his hands up defensively with a soft chuckle. "My father insisted I come here tonight. When I saw your fake smile, I admit I was intrigued. Most women in Capital Hill would flourish at the attention, but you looked uncomfortable."

"I can't tell if you're honestly giving me a compliment or if you're making fun of me."

"Compliment. I want to get to know you better Alice. From this conversation, I can tell you're more grounded than other women, and I appreciate that. If you take time to get to know me, you'll discover we have much in common."

The words to turn down his offer were on my tongue. A voice projected from the parlour room announcing dinner. My mother came into the sunroom looking for me. When she spotted Lucas, her lips formed an 'O' shape, and she promptly left us. I quickly followed her to the dining room, needing to get away. Lucas followed close behind me. He pulled a chair out for me in the dining room, then sat to my left.

Something about Lucas set off warning bells in the back of my mind. His pale green eyes were unnervingly familiar, yet I'd never seen Lucas before. I wish I could pinpoint the exact reason behind the unease. He made small talk with me during dinner, which I countered with short one or two-worded answers. I could feel my mother's pride further down the table. She would say this party was a success once the guests were gone.

After dinner, the men ventured to the drawing room for brandy while the women returned to the parlour. Fortunately, the young men who were specifically invited to be introduced to me had followed their fathers. I was not looking forward to sitting in the parlour for idle gossip with the other women, especially since it'll be the mothers prying to see what I think of their sons.

Lucas gently took hold of my elbow. "Let's go somewhere quiet."

"I'd rather not." I pulled my arm away.

"Afraid to be alone with me?" He teased.

"Absolutely not!"

"Prove it." He grinned playfully.

I bit my cheek. He was calling my courage into question. I shouldn't give in to the teasing, but my pride won't let me back down. So, shoulders back, I led him to the game room. This room has a card table, a pool table, and a TV for video games and sporting events, with couches and chairs around the massive screen.

"Quiet enough for you?"

Lucas closed the door and stalked toward me. "Much better."

I mirrored his steps backward until I hit the pool table. "What are you doing?"

"I enjoyed our conversation tonight, Alice. You were a little distant at dinner. I assumed that was because there were so many eyes on us."

"I'm not interested in getting to know you better." I countered firmly.

He smiled. "Maybe this will change your mind."

Before I realized what he'd meant, Lucas was kissing me. His hands cupped my face as he pressed his body closer to mine. I reached behind me, searching for something on the pool table surface to use as a defensive weapon. My hand wrapped around an object. I brought the item down on the side of his head.

Lucas growled, a mixture of irritation and pain. He stepped back, holding his head as he glared at the object in my hand. I glanced at the triangle in my hand. The pool cue would have been better. At least with it, I could keep Lucas at a distance. Dropping the triangle, I quickly skirted around Lucas. He reached out to grab me, but I twisted out of his reach and ran out of the room. Lucas called after me. I didn't stop until I nearly flew into Francine, one of our maids. The woman stared blankly into one of the two libraries in the house.

"Francine?" I asked, but the woman didn't respond. "What are you looking at?"

"Alice." Lucas took hold of my arm when he caught up with me.

"Call the police."

I stared wide-eyed at the dead body in the library. Blood was staining the front of the man's shirt, and his head tilted forward, obscuring the view of his wound. I yanked my arm from his grip.

"Lucas, call the police now!"

Lucas looked confused and then peered into the room. His eyes widened. I had to give him credit. He didn't appear as though he was going to be sick at the sight of the dead body. I called his name again. He shook his head, pulled his phone from his pants pocket, and dialled 9-1-1. I turned my focus to Francine; the woman wore a glazed expression. This is an expression I've seen on humans when a vampire takes over their minds. I've seen Queen do it to her human servants for my benefit. Which means there's a vampire in my house.

Lucas hung up on the police. I urged Lucas to inform my father of the murder. He argued he shouldn't leave me alone with a murderer in the house. I gritted my teeth, annoyed that he was trying to protect me when he had just forced a kiss on me. I insisted my father had to know and that I'd stay with Francine. Lucas hesitated, glancing at the maid but nodded anyway.

Once he was out of sight, I ran upstairs. I need to find the vampire. I need a weapon. I also need to call Ryan. As a detective, he'd have a reason to be here. As the Alpha of the Stellacote wolf pack, he'd be my best hope of helping me take out the vampire. I'd call Queen Ana later; her arrival now would be out of place.

There's no way this vampire is one of the Queen's. She keeps her vampires in line. I've never had to hunt a vampire because of the Sanguis — Queen's special warrior vampire enforcers. They handle any troublemakers before news reaches my ears.

I grabbed my phone off the desk in my room. My heart raced as it rang. I mentally prayed it wouldn't go to voice mail. Relief eased the tension in my body when the call was answered.

"Detective Lune." The deep voice sent a pleasurable shiver down my spine.

I shook my head, needing to concentrate on my reason for calling. "Ryan."

"Alice?" He questioned, sounding surprised.

I didn't answer him immediately. Feeling someone watching me, I turned slowly to see a tall, golden-blond-haired man with glowing blue eyes staring at me. My body tensed. I didn't grab a weapon before calling Ryan. The man smiled, revealing his pointed fangs. My blood chilled upon seeing him, and my words came out choppy and rushed.

"Murder. My house. Va-ahh!"

I screamed as the vampire rushed me, knocking my phone out of my hands. He then grabbed me by the neck. With a single hand, he lifted me off the ground. I struggled in his grip, nails clawing at his hand, trying to separate his fingers from my neck as my toes scraped the floor. My vision blurred. Memories of my father showing me how to break free skittered across my mind — unfortunately, this is a vampire, not a human. It won't be so easy to break his hold.

I forced myself to stop struggling and fall limp in his hold while holding my breath. The vampire put me on my feet, shifting his grip to my shoulders to keep me upright. I could feel the vampire's breath on my skin as he leaned into my neck. I won't go down without a fight. With as much strength as I could muster, I slammed my palm under his chin, forcing his head away. Then I ducked down, pivoting from under his arm and stumbled toward my bedside table. Taking big gulps of air, I struggled to open the drawer.

He rubbed his jaw, smiling at the silver blade I now held. "Found you."

Between the chokehold and me holding my breath, there wasn't enough oxygen in my brain to react quickly. He came at me again. I barely dodged to the side while swiping the blade at him. With the heels and dress, my movements were even more hampered. Using my bed as leverage, the vampire pounced on me. Knocking me to the floor. I got a slash across his chest before he grabbed my wrist and slammed it into the floor, forcing me to let go of the blade.

"You're mine Hunter."

He sat kneeling between my legs, my wrists held on either side of my head. The vampire licked his lips, staring at my neck. My pulse quickened. He was going to bite me. My mind raced, trying to figure out how to free myself. Spreading my legs further apart — challenging with my dress caught under his knee — I brought my feet up and dug the heels of my shoes into his sides. The vampire howled in pain, drawing back.

Grabbing my ankles, he shoved me away violently. I slid through the French doors, my back hitting the concrete balustrades of my balcony. Pain ran through me. The vampire watched me struggle to sit up as he pulled the shoes from his sides. The wounds healed instantly. The vampire stalked over to me furiously.

"You will be worth all this trouble." He growled.

Pinning my arms to my side, he lifted me to my feet and pressed himself against me. I was pinned between the balcony and the vampire. His fangs pierced the skin of my neck. I screamed. As quickly as he bit me, he pulled away. I don't know why, and I don't care — at least not now.

The vampire vanished. No longer being held up by him, I slid down. My hand covered my neck. I need to get this cleaned.

"Alice!"

Lucas knelt in front of me. Fear was evident in his features. He put an arm around my waist and threw my other arm over his shoulders. Lucas helped me to stand and brought me back into my bedroom.

Ryan picked that moment to burst into my room. My heart fluttered at the sight of him.

"Ryan."

"Miss Thorpe." His voice sounded strained. "Are you okay?"

— · —

# Chapter Three

## Ryan

My attention was split between my concern for Alice and my hatred for the unknown man. The man held Alice's arm around his neck, and his other arm wrapped around her waist. He held her too close. My hands clenched at my side as I struggled to keep my wolf from taking over and tearing him limb from limb. Once under control, I forced myself to focus on Alice and only on Alice. She looked pale and held her neck with her free hand. I feared the worst had happened after her call dropped. Now I fear I may be too late.

"Miss Thorpe?" I repeated.

"She was just attacked!" The man's grip on her tightened. "Do you think she's okay?"

"I wasn't asking you, sir." I ground out, trying to maintain my composure.

"Lucas." He stated, squaring his shoulders as if he was important. "Alice needs medical attention."

"Ryan." Alice's breathy tone drew both of our attention. "The body."

"Bret will return shortly." I couldn't take my eyes off her neck. She had to have been bit. I scooped her out of Lucas's hold and into my arms in two long strides. She feels right in my arms. "Right now, you're my top priority."

"Hey!" Lucas protested. "Who the hell are you?"

"Detective Ryan Lune."

"Where are you going?"

"She needs medical attention." I threw his own words back at him.

I rushed out of the room. I need to treat her wound before she succumbs to the vampire's bite. Alice's eyes fluttered shut. Not good. I jostled her in my arms. I can't lose her, not like this.

"Stay awake." I demanded softly.

"It's so hard." She admitted curling into me.

Bret stepped into the house as we neared the bottom of the stairs. His eyes first found the crowd of people. Then, with a frown, he took in Alice's worsening state. "I'll handle things here. Go."

With a thankful nod to my partner, I rushed past him to get to my car. Lucas slipped into the back seat as I carefully placed Alice. I don't have time to argue with him. Sirens on, I drove away from the Thorpe house as other cop cars were pulled in. I need to get Alice to the station. I need to cleanse the bite. In the past, every bitten human I've encountered has died from an untreated vampire bite. Alice won't be one of those humans.

"This isn't the way to the hospital." Lucas noted.

"Keep her awake!" I ordered.

I purposefully hit the edge of potholes to jolt Alice awake. Lucas would tap her cheek when her eyes drifted, but it didn't last long. She was fading fast. My blood boiled when I glanced in the rear-view mirror and saw him kissing her. It worked. Alice's eyes were wide open. I hit the brakes hard as I parked in my spot, jostling them both forward.

I flung the back door open, pulling Alice away from Lucas. I carried her to the basement. Lucas tried to keep up but was stopped at the front desk. I shifted Alice in my arms to fish the keys out of my pocket to unlock the door blocking my path. Very few people know what lies behind this door, and only those few have keys.

This basement room almost looks like a bathroom. There's a tub and a sink with a water tank, not linked to the rest of the station, filled with Holy Water, a couch, and a cabinet. The room was made to be soundproof because cleansing a vampire's bite is far from painless. I kicked the door shut, turning to flip the bolt. I gently placed Alice on the couch before banging erupted on the other side. Lucas caught up. Ignoring him, I grabbed a bucket from the cabinet and filled it in the tub. I set the bucket next to the couch, grabbed a cup and a towel, then knelt beside Alice.

"This is going to hurt." I warned.

Dipping the cup into the bucket, I poured the Holy Water over the wound. Alice screamed at the pain, arching off the couch. I put an arm over her to hold her in place as I poured more water on her neck. The wound bubbled. Alice writhed beneath me. Wiping at the wound with the towel, I poured a fresh cup of water over it. Her screams hurt both my sensitive ears and my heart.

It took fifteen to twenty minutes before Alice stopped thrashing beneath my hold. I cleaned up the wound, pouring yet another cup of Holy Water. Alice hissed her annoyance at me, her body tensing. I continued until the bite stopped bubbling and wiped at her neck to verify that the Holy Water had done its job to my satisfaction. It took a bucket and a half until I could no longer see the two red puncture marks that had marred her skin.

"Can you sit up?"

She forced herself a little higher on the couch. "Sort of. My back really, really hurts."

"Drink this." I filled the cup a final time.

"What will it do?" Alice eyed the water.

"The Holy Water will cleanse your insides." When her nose scrunched up adorably at the explanation, I chuckled. "Don't worry. It won't hurt. Think of it as extra insurance that you're purified."

"I'm far from pure."

"You're purer than the monsters you hunt."

Alice took the water. "You're not a monster Ryan."

"You haven't seen me on a full moon." I mumbled.

Once the cup was empty, I took it from her, cleaning up the bucket and towel. Turning back, I took in Alice's appearance. She had slid back down on the couch, her eyes closed. Her brown hair stuck to her sweat-soaked skin, and her make-up looked like it was melting off her face. Somehow the dress seemed to have survived the attack. My eyes roamed the length of her body, appreciating what it did to her. It hugged her so perfectly that not much was left to the imagination. Her breathing was heavy as she tried to regain her composure, causing her chest to rise and fall. Her breasts nearly fell out of the dress with each intake. The skirt portion fell off the couch, the high slit exposing her long legs. I swallowed hard.

"Thank you Ryan."

I drew my eyes back to hers. Gorgeous brown eyes stared back at me. I sat heavily on the floor near her head, exhaustion hitting me. I nearly lost her tonight. The monsters she hunts almost took our my strong, beautiful, stubborn Hunter by a worse monster than me. Alice Thorpe has buried herself so deep in my heart that losing her would be like losing a part of myself. Not that I deserve to feel this way.

"What happened?" I forced the question out.

"The vampire attacked me when I was calling you about the murder. I tried to fight back, but he was strong. I thought I was done for when I went through the window and hit the balcony."

She winced, turning on her side to face me. She's physically injured too. A strong urge to strip her down, check every inch of her body, and kiss her injuries better filled me. I had to shake the tempting and dangerous thought from my mind. I doubt she'd want another monster to touch her tonight or ever again.

"That vampire threw me around like a rag doll."

There was a soft, constant knock on the door. I growled, glaring in that direction. "How does Lucas fit in?"

Alice frowned. "He's a guest of Mother's match-making event."

"Match-making?"

I refocused on her. My stomach churned at the thought of her being with someone else. I know she'll find someone eventually to settle down with, and I have no right to stop her from finding the person she wants to be with. But, even knowing all that, it doesn't stop me from hating the idea of her being with someone who is not me.

"I was against it."

"That's." I struggled to find an appropriate word. "Old fashioned."

"Lucas has decided I'm the one for him."

"And you? What have you decided?" My breath held for her answer.

Alice smiled softly, tentatively. "My heart flutters for another."

My wolf, and I, relaxed at her answer. I don't feel like a monster when I'm with Alice, but deep down, I know that's not reality. I brushed my fingers along her cheek. Leaning in, I kissed her gently. The soft caress of lips is not enough. I edged forward, pressing my lips more firmly onto hers, needing to know she was okay. Alice slid her hand to my neck, kissing me back with as much fervour. My ringing cell phone stopped me from going further.

"Rest." I ordered, my lips brushing along hers before I pulled away.

I stayed with Alice until she fell asleep. Then, I pulled a notepad out of my back pocket, scribbled a message for her, and taped it to the door with medical tape from the cabinet. This note should ease her mind if she wakes up before I can return. Then, exiting the room, I kicked Lucas awake and out of my way so I could get out.

"Go home." I ordered as the boy groaned awake.

He looked up at me, blinking the sleep away. "Alice?"

"She's resting."

"Let me see her!"

"She's resting." I growled while keeping a tight hold on the door-knob. "Go home."

"Not until I see that she's all right."

I grabbed Lucas's arm leading him back up to the main floor. "Miss Thorpe is fine. She needs time to rest — in peace. If she cares to tell you about her condition when she wakes, she'll do just that. I'll let her know of your concern."

Lucas scowled. "No, you won't."

"You're right. I won't." I answered dryly, eyes catching sight of the junior detective yawning at his desk. "Baxter!"

He jumped, startled, then came rushing over. "Yes detective?"

"Make sure Lucas gets home." I shoved the boy forward. "Get a few hours of rest and return in the morning ready to work."

"Yes, sir!" He saluted, taking hold of Lucas's arm.

"I'm not going anywhere until I see Alice." Lucas protested.

Frustrated, I gave him an ultimatum. "You want to stay? Fine, you can wait in the holding cells."

"You have no right to do that!"

"You are not Miss Thorpe's family; therefore, you have no right to see her while she's resting. The longer you argue with me, the more you obstruct the case to find the perpetrator who attacked Miss Thorpe."

Lucas fell silent. His lips thinned as he contemplated his next move. Thankfully he didn't argue this time. Instead, he allowed Baxter to lead him out of the station with a nod. I ran a hand over my face. The mixture of worry, relief, annoyance, and exhaustion are starting to take its toll.

Turning, I marched to the captain's office. The captain's door was open. I knocked and entered. He had called earlier for an update, but I refused to leave Alice's side until I was sure she'd fallen asleep.

"How's the Capital Hill case coming?"

I closed the door to prevent prying ears from listening in. "We've determined it's a vampire."

Hugh growled, disgust clear in the sound. I couldn't blame him.

He had witnessed an enraged vampire in his first year as captain. I shot the vampire, forcing him back from the man, but Queen and her Sanguis killed it. At the time, I had convinced Queen not to wipe Hugh's memories, claiming it would be easier to work the supernatural cases if the boss knew what was happening. It took some persuading, but Queen agreed — reluctantly. She threatened Hugh that he'd no longer have a pulse if word got out about vampires and he was the source.

After that incident, Bret and I created the basement room for emergencies. Thank goodness we did. I have no idea what I would have done if I couldn't save Alice from the vampire's bite.

"Have you talked to the vampire leader?"

"She's been ignoring me." I scowled. "I plan on going to visit her tomorrow. But first, I want to collect evidence so she can't deny what is happening in Stellacote."

Hugh's grey eyes softened. "And the girl who was attacked?"

"Miss Thorpe will make a full recovery."

"Good. When she's ready, take her statement and catch this killer."

I nodded and left his office. Even more determined to catch this vampire, I went straight to my shared corner office. Bret was pinning photos of the Colt and Thorpe houses on our corkboard. I stood beside my Beta. We've never been able to figure out a connection between any of these murders, aside from the general location of Capital Hill. Strings connected the images of the victims with the site of their murder. I ran my finger from the first house to the second, third and fourth — the Thorpe residence. Always three people; a man, a woman, and a younger woman. My eyes kept falling onto Alice's picture, the answer coming to me.

"Hunters!"

"Excuse me?" Bret questioned, a brow raising above his glasses.

"The Thorpe family, the Hunters for Stellacote, are a family of three." I pointed to each of the other murder locations. "The people might not be related, but it's symbolic. The vampire was looking for the Hunter, and he killed three people each time. So, it has to be a message that he is aiming for her whole family."

Bret's eyes widened as understanding filled them. "The vampire was toying with the Hunter. He knew exactly where to find them."

"If that's true, why did he attack her tonight?"

He followed the path from each crime scene using another string, forming a reverse star. "Unless we're reading this all wrong."

"What are the chances other Hunters haven't been targeted?" I sat at my desk, calling various Alphas across the country, each informing me that their Hunter was fine and no vampire had attacked their city. "Nothing."

"Aren't the Thorpe's founding members of the Hunter Society? Or at least Hunter leaders?" Bret questioned. "Maybe this is about cutting the snake's head off."

I raised a questioning brow. That was a term I don't think I've ever heard before. "Meaning?"

"It means. if you remove the leader, then its subjects will be weak."

"You're thinking this is political?"

"It's an option. If the Hunter Society leaders are gone, the Hunters below them lack guidance and protection. The more radical Hunters won't have anyone holding them back from attacking the supernatural. Also, the supernatural won't have to fear that the Hunters will come for them if they attack first. This vampire is bringing us closer to war, closer to how it used to be."

"That military mind of yours is scary." I shivered. "I'll call Charlie. I know a Hunter leader is in Australia. Possibly even in his area."

"G'day, mate." Charlie answered cheerfully.

"Charlie, it's Ryan." No time for pleasantries. I got straight to the point. "I need to know if the Hunter Society leader in Australia has been attacked."

There was silence on the other end before Charlie sighed reluctantly. "Bloody oath. Roman warned me the Hunter family would be up a gumtree. But, bad trot, I was too late. The Hunters lived in the back of Bourke. When we got there, they up and disappeared."

"Disappeared?" I could never understand some of his terms, but I could pick up keywords.

"All five of them. We tracked the scents but had to give it away."

"Scents?"

"Wolves. Vamps. Aussies."

My heart sank at the thought of Alice disappearing. "Thanks, Charlie."

"Hooroo."

Bret waited for me to hang up the phone. "Did you say disappear?"

I didn't bother acknowledging the question. My Beta would have heard the conversation. "As concerning as that is, I'm more intrigued with Roman. Why did he warn Charlie and not me? How did he even know he had to warn Charlie?"

"Maybe he didn't know about the Thorpe's." Bret suggested weakly. "But it is something to look into."

I was already dialling the European Alpha before he even finished speaking. Europe is so large that there are two main Alphas in that continent. Roman is one of the scariest Alphas I've ever met. We crossed paths when I was still a young wolf, visiting France. At the time, I struggled to be one with my wolf. Roman had recently become Alpha by killing the previous one in a dominant fight. Rumours around the wolf are that he used to be a Russian Special Forces member before he was turned in a mission gone wrong.

I cursed as the ringing went to voice mail. I left a short, curt message and then slammed the phone down. I need to know what Roman knows so I can protect Alice. I grabbed my keys leaving the office. I need to run, clear my mind, and express my frustrations.

I drove out of Stellacote to where trees lined the roads in thick clusters blocking the view of the massive old houses. I turned off the main road onto a dirt road leading to my first house. I lived here before Stellacote became the city it is now. I moved into the city to be closer to my job. This house is kept in working order for my pack. Because it is so well hidden, they can shift and run around without fear of being caught. The supernatural monsters like to stay hidden, so Hunters won't be able to hunt them down so easily.

About a dozen of my pack are living in the house right now. Those who are restless or too new to be trusted to live in the city, and a few who prefer the quiet. I parked along the side of the house closest to the woods. Getting out, I stripped out of my clothes to not ruin them during my shift.

I tilted my head toward the moon allowing its power to pull my wolf out. Going from human to wolf is a painful process that takes time. I used to scream every time I shifted during a full moon. Now that I'm more used to the pain, it doesn't affect me as strongly as it used to.

After shifting, I shook my head, clearing it of any lingering pain. Then I took off for the woods. The Earth beneath my paws, the wind through my fur, running as a wolf feels freeing. The case still ran through my mind, my need to protect Alice urging me faster as anger over her attack blinded me. Finally, I let out a frustrated howl.

I probably would have seen the connection sooner if Roman had warned me as he did Charlie. I attacked the tree that blocked my path, lunging at it, snapping it from its vertical position. If I had told Alice about the Capital Hill attacks, she would have been more prepared when the vampire went after her. I hate that Alice was put into danger like that, because of me, because I couldn't catch this vampire sooner. I never want her in that danger again. I growled. As a Hunter, Alice will always be in danger. I need to figure out how to protect her best.

# Chapter Four

## Alice

My head throbbed. The pain in my back sent shockwaves through my body. I groaned, rolling to my side to get the weight off my back, only to fall face-first from where I lay. An expletive slipped past my lips. Opening my eyes, I pushed myself to my knees and looked around. The memory of the blond vampire biting me had me reaching for my neck in search of the injury. I felt nothing. Getting to my feet, I wobbled, trying to find my balance and stumbled over to the mirror. No mark marred my skin. Looking around the room, I noticed a piece of paper taped to the only door. Putting my arms out for balance, I slowly walked over to read it.

*Alice*

*You're in the basement of the police station. Last night I cleansed the vampire bite. There's a trusted cop just beyond the door who can take you home. I will catch the vampire that bit you. For now, you should rest.*

*Ryan*

I flushed. A vague memory of a kiss with Ryan flashed in my mind as I read the note. I can't remember if it happened or if it was just a lingering dream. I re-read the note. There's no way I'll let Ryan go after this vampire without me. The creature bit me. I deserve the right to track him down. I'm a Hunter after all. It's my job to track down dangerous supernatural creatures and take care of them. I looked down at myself, still wearing the dress from my mother's match-making party. Not suitable for hunting. First, I'll go home, freshen up, and then return to talk to Ryan.

Just as the note had instructed, an officer stood waiting for me on the other side of the door. He led me upstairs and out into the sun with a kind smile. He didn't pry over my attire or why I was in the basement. Instead, he kept a kind smile on his face and his eyes on the road as he drove.

"Here you are Miss Thorpe." He put the car in park. "I'll inform Detective Lune that you're home safe."

"That won't be necessary. I'll be returning shortly to discuss my attacker." I got out, but before closing the door popped my head back inside. "Thank you for the drive home."

He sat in the driveway, watching me. I had to ring the doorbell to be let in. My key is in my room, and I am not about to use the spare key with the officer sitting there. Thankfully our head butler — Lynol — was prompt in answering the door. I heard the car depart as I stepped into the house.

"Miss Thorpe." He greeted with relief. "It's good to see you."

"You too Lynol. Do you mind preparing me some toast and jam? I'm going to freshen up."

"Not at all Miss."

"Alice?" My mother came rushing down the hall and pulled me into a hug. "Where were you last night? There was a murder, and the police came, and you were nowhere to be found."

"I was attacked and taken to be checked out."

"That young man you were with last night must have saved you and taken you to the hospital. That's good to hear." Her worry for me washed away instantly. "Remind me, what's his name?"

I frowned, knowing correcting her on the situation would only have her worried again. "Do you mean Lucas?"

"Did you not get his last name?"

"No Mother."

She clicked her tongue. "Never you mind, I'll find out."

"Vivian, honey." My father joined us in the entryway. "Let your daughter freshen up."

"Of course." My mother smiled brightly.

I smiled at my father. I rushed upstairs as quickly as I dared. My bare feet hurt. Grabbing more comfortable clothes, I moved to the bathroom. Stripping out of the dress, I turned to peer at my back in the mirror: a large bruise was beginning to colour my skin. I popped two ibuprofen in my mouth and then hopped into the shower.

The hot water helped ease my sore muscles, but I suspected I would be stiff for a while. Feeling refreshed, I dressed and returned to my room while running my fingers through my hair to remove any knots. Someone knocked on my door, entering only when I answered. My father walked in with a plate holding two pieces of toast smothered in butter and jam.

"Tell me what happened last night." He handed me the plate.

I sat on the bed and took a couple of bites before starting the brief explanation. "A blond vampire attacked me. He bit me. If Ryan — I mean Detective Lune didn't arrive when he did." I shivered. "I don't even want to imagine that situation."

"Why was Detective Lune here?"

"I called him." I ate half the toast before answering my father's questioning gaze. "I found Francine staring at the body in the library with a glazed expression. I suspected it was due to a vampire, so I came here to call Detective Lune and get a weapon. That's when the vampire attacked me."

My father paced before me, a hand on his chin, the other behind his back. I ate my toast in silence. I may be the active Hunter for Stellacote, but my father is still a prominent member of the Hunter Society. The society communicates with each other often, and he receives those messages. He stays apprised of everything that goes on within the society. But, to my displeasure, he keeps me out of the politics. I want to learn everything there is to know about being a Hunter, including its politics, but my father refuses to teach me.

"I want you to always have a weapon on you and be weary of your surroundings when you go out." He ordered. "Something about this situation seems off."

"I will Father." I set the plate down beside me. "Will you be reaching out to the society?"

He nodded, stopping to turn to me. "That boy you were with."

"Lucas?" I frowned. "I want nothing to do with him. He set off warning bells."

"Good." He nodded again.

"Mother seems to like him."

"Let her play matchmaker. It makes her happy. I won't let you go down the wedding aisle unless your groom is someone you love." He stared at me with a severe expression. "Keep your wits about you."

"I will."

I suspect he knows something more about this situation. If I press for details, he'll only push me away. The best I can do now is wait for the answers to reveal themselves by finding them myself.

"I'm going to stop by the station to see what Detective Lune can tell me about last night's attack."

"Good idea." He agreed.

Smiling softly, he kissed my forehead before leaving the room. I returned to the bathroom, brushed my teeth, and put my hair into a ponytail. I grabbed the plate, my phone — which surprisingly survived the attack — and my key. My driver's license and credit card are hidden in the phone case, so I never have to carry a purse. They are troublesome things that get in the way of my fighting. Though if they have enough weight to them, they can also be good one-time weapons to disorient an attacker with a single blow to the head.

Before heading downstairs, I slipped into my father's study. Putting the plate down on the desk, I pushed the grandfather clock that stood against an inner wall to the side, revealing a spiral stone staircase. At the bottom is the weapons and training room where I spent most of my youth. There is no way I am leaving this house without weapons. I stopped at the first weapons table, sliding daggers into sheaths sewn inside my boots, then moved to the hidden weapon table.

I scanned the small table, deciding what to wear. Finally, I slid a silver bracelet with a rose on my wrist. Designed after a 19th-century snake bracelet, a thirty-one-inch rapier blade is revealed when I pull on the rose. For the day, this is all I'll need — I hope.

Returning to the study, I put the clock back in place and picked up the plate again. This time I carried it to the kitchen, where my mother sat reviewing lists of names. I don't dare ask her what she's doing, afraid of the answer.

"I'm going to the police station." I announced.

"That's an excellent idea." She smiled at me. "I'll come with you."

"That's not necessary."

"Nonsense. I'll ask the captain to add officers around our house. If your attacker returns, I want to be prepared."

Usually, that would be a good idea, but my attacker is a vampire, and human guards won't be able to do anything to stop him if he comes back. My mother grabbed the purse she leaves near the garage, fishing for her car keys. I followed silently. I would much prefer going alone, but there's no arguing when my mother stubbornly makes a decision.

Once at the station, my mother was guided to the captain's office. Partway there, I saw the officer who took me home and informed her that I needed to give a statement about the attack. Only a partial lie. She glanced at the officer I was pointing to and reluctantly allowed me to leave her side.

I waited for my mother to continue down the hall and turn the corner before I slipped away to Ryan's office. Technically an officer should guide me, but I don't have the luxury of following procedure.

I need to talk to Ryan before my mother finishes her conversation with the captain. Besides, I know where I'm going anyway.

Ryan, and his partner Bret, share an enclosed office space in the back corner of the building. I knocked on the open door and poked my head inside to see no one was around. Ryan's desk sat closest to the exterior windows, covered in paperwork and stacks of files. Between the two desks in the room sat a corkboard with a map of Capital Hill and other various notes pinned to it. Bret's desk, situated opposite Ryan's near the inner wall of the station, was perfectly well-kept. I stepped closer to the corkboard.

"Miss Thorpe."

I jumped, a hand on my wrist ready to pull out the rapier. Bret stood behind me. "You startled me."

"My apologies." He took in my stance, then handed me one of the two mugs he held. "An herbal peppermint tea. It should help you relax."

"Thank you." I took it, breathing in the minty scent. "Where's Ryan?"

"He went out for some fresh air last night. I haven't seen him yet this morning."

"Do you think he'll be back soon?"

His lips quirked. "I can call him."

"There's no need to rush him."

I returned my attention to the cork board sipping my tea — or rather, grass-flavoured water. I much prefer coffee. Bret is right though. I find the peppermint relaxing. Hands wrapped around the warm mug, I savoured the scent more than the flavour.

"Tough case?"

"Yes."

His exasperated tone had me glancing over my shoulder at him, catching him as he pushed up his glasses to rub the bridge of his nose. I noted how tired he looked. Bret closed the office door. We are alone. The blinds in the windows facing the station are drawn so there are no prying eyes. Even the blinds for the exterior windows are partially drawn. I don't mind being in the same room as him. Bret gives off a calming aura.

I watched him out of the corner of my eye as he sat at his desk, sipped his mug, opened a file, and began to read. He looks approximately twenty-nine, with short dirty blond hair and hazel eyes. Since he's a wolf, I know he's much older than he looks, but if the average human met him, they'd think he's very mature.

"Is there something you'd like to ask me Miss Thorpe?" Bret inquired, not looking up from his file.

"How old were you when you changed?"

"Twenty-nine."

I smiled, proud that I'd guessed correctly.

"Why do you ask?"

"Just curious." I shrugged, moving to sit in the chair across from him. "What about Ryan?"

"Thirty-two." He looked up at me from above his glasses. "Any other questions about my Alpha, and you'd have to ask him personally."

I hid behind my mug of tea, feeling my cheeks warm. His hazel eyes twinkled with a knowing glint as if he knew why I was asking about Ryan. I cleared my throat, shifting my attention back to the corkboard as I curled my legs under me in the chair. Images of the victims are pinned in groups of three with a single date and a string between them and their houses. I frowned, studying the board. They are all recent. I subconsciously sipped my tea, eyes flickering across every victim.

"Why didn't you tell me about the vampire sooner?"

"It was not my place to say."

My eyes narrowed on a piece of paper with my last name and the date of the attack. "Why didn't Ryan tell me?"

"You'll have to ask him."

I shifted back around, placing my feet on the floor and winced at the too-hard impact running up my spine. "I was attacked in my own home because I wasn't informed. I could have been more prepared if I'd known."

Bret eyed me. "How badly were you injured?"

"I was injured because I wasn't prepared."

"There is nothing I can tell you, Miss Thorpe."

I stood, walking over to the corkboard. "These victims could have been saved."

"He was looking for you." Ryan growled, slamming the door shut as he entered the room.

"I know that already." I countered, turning to him.

Ryan's brown hair was wet as if he ran through the shower, the stubble along his jaw longer than usual. His brown eyes seemed to have a golden glow as if he was struggling to keep his wolf hidden, but the wild animal was just too close to the surface. He was in the middle of buttoning up his dress shirt. My gaze flickered down to his exposed chest, blushing. Finally, I averted my gaze to the floor and sipped more tea. Ryan finished buttoning his shirt before speaking.

"What do you mean: you know?"

I looked up. His voice was dangerously low. I had never heard that tone in him before. It sent a shiver down my spine. Not one of fear. I wondered if he used that tone while intimate with a woman. It was demanding and sexy. I shook out my wondering thoughts and frowned.

"The vampire spoke to me. Said: found you, and you're mine Hunter." I didn't bother telling them the last thing he said. It didn't make sense to me.

His eyes flashed golden yellow, the promise of murder in their depth. His words were spoken through gritted teeth. "You are not his."

"What can you tell us about the vampire?" Bret stood and came around his desk, his body tense.

"I remember." I closed my eyes, drawing the vampire's face in my mind. "He has golden-blond hair and glowing blue eyes."

"Any defining features?"

I shook my head, opening my eyes. "I panicked when I saw him. I've never fought a vampire before. It was only during our fight did he speak to me."

"We will bring that description to Queen."

I looked at him, startled. "Have you not spoken to her about this vampire?"

"I've tried." Ryan ran a hand down his face. "She shut me down last time, claiming she knows nothing about these murders."

"Let me talk to her."

"No!"

I placed the mug down on Bret's desk before I decided to throw it at him. "Queen has never turned me down and has never lied to me. I will talk to her tonight."

"Going out with this vampire out there is too dangerous."

"It's more dangerous staying at home where he can easily find me."

"She has a point." Bret spoke up, maintaining a spot between us like a peacekeeper. "If the Hunter can get Queen to talk, then why don't you go with her?"

Ryan glared at Bret. "That's not the point."

"What is your point?" I accused. "Lock me up like some damsel so you can be the hero?"

Ryan flushed. "No. That's not. Alice."

He stumbled over his words but never got the chance to explain. My mother flew the door open in a panic, shoving Ryan aside to get to me. I groaned as she wrapped her arms tightly around me. I am going to need more ibuprofen when I get home. Worry washed over my mother's features, which turned to anger as she stepped back.

"I was so worried when you weren't with the officer giving your statement. He said you had never gone to him after you left my side."

"Mother, I'm in a police station, and you have the car keys." I tried to explain calmly. "Where would I go?"

My mother huffed. She looked between Ryan and Bret, then back to me. "Why are you with these men?"

"Detectives Lune and Michaelson are working on finding my attacker."

"Miss Thorpe was kind enough to offer some details to aid our search." Bret offered her a charming smile. "You have a courageous daughter."

My mother blushed. "While you two search for her attacker, Captain Forest offered protection for our house."

Ryan smiled politely. "May we offer our assistance as well? My partner and I can take shifts personally protecting Miss Thorpe."

I glared at him. "I don't want you to fall behind on your investigation."

"What if your attacker returns while you're away from the house?"

"Oh my! I haven't thought of that." My mother brought a hand to her mouth, eyes widening. "Would protecting my daughter interrupt your investigation?"

"The safety of Miss Thorpe is our top priority."

"Then I accept your assistance. Your dedication is most appreciated Detective Lune." My mother took my hand. "Come, Alice, let's get you home."

"I'll be over later tonight." Ryan called after us as we left his office.

I mentally battled with this new situation. Part of me hated that I was about to have a bodyguard. Another part of me was thrilled Ryan would be my personal guard. How easily Bret and Ryan had charmed my mother was another concern. Perhaps my mother's mental state has made her too vulnerable. It doesn't matter now; she already agreed to their offer to protect me personally. I wonder what my father will think about the Alpha and Beta of Stellacote becoming my bodyguards.

I'm beginning to feel like my status of Hunter means nothing. My father doesn't tell me anything. Ryan keeps things from me. He probably thinks of me as a weak human that needs protection. I'll prove him wrong. I'll get information out of Queen that he hasn't been able to get. I'll also track down this vampire before he does. I'm not weak, and I'm not useless. I am a Hunter, and I'm good at what I do.

# Chapter Five

## Ryan

The sun had risen during my run, replacing the moon in the sky. Returning to the car, I shifted back. The run didn't help as much as I had hoped, but it let my wolf and myself remove some frustration. Returning to the station, I went to the locker room for a shower and a fresh shirt. I paused while buttoning up my shirt as I approached my office. Alice's voice came from just beyond the door.

"These victims could have been saved." Alice claimed.

I stormed into the office, slamming the door behind me. "He was looking for you."

"I know that already."

She turned to me, her eyes widening slightly when they met mine. I know my wolf is still sitting near the surface. I can feel it, and she must see the monster within. A twinge of regret pained me. I never want her scared of me. Her eyes then ran down my body, a blush coating her cheeks. Unable to return to meet my gaze, she focussed instead on the floor. I frowned, finished buttoning my shirt, then spoke.

"What do you mean: you know?"

She explained that the vampire spoke to her and briefly described the vampire. I heard her talking, heard myself and Bret speak to her, but I couldn't focus. Too many emotions and thoughts split my attention. I almost lost Alice last night, and I couldn't get that fear from my mind. She's good at hiding her pain, but I could see that the attack shook her and that she was trying to hide any physical pain from the attack. I want to soothe any lingering fear and promise her that I'll protect her. But I can't.

The topic of her attacker brought up Queen's name, and she seemed to straighten her spine. Her suggestion of visiting the city's vampire ruler is out of the question. We argued. The verbal debate was a relief to my nerves. It means, to me at least, that she won't let this attack turn her into a frightened little bunny. Her strong will is still present even after the attack. My fear of losing her caused my mouth to say something stupid before my brain had time to register the words.

"What is your point?" Alice bit out. "Lock me up like some damsel so you can be the hero?"

"No." I stammered. I was trying and failing to backtrack my previously poorly chosen words. "That's not. Alice."

The idea of being her hero is sensational, but that's not what Alice wants. Not what she needs. She wants to prove that she's strong and has earned her place as a Hunter. I want to keep her safe but don't want to stop her from fighting. As much as my wolf disagrees with that. I don't want her going into danger by herself. I want to be by her side, helping her.

I don't even get a chance to explain myself adequately when her mother bursts into the room. I watched the woman hug her daughter tightly, causing Alice to wince, then began complaining that she wasn't where she said she'd be. I bit my tongue. I want to tell her that Alice doesn't need to inform her of her every movement. But it's not my place to say anything. When Mrs. Thorpe suddenly mentioned Captain Forest offering house protection, I perked up, giving me an idea of how to protect Alice. The woman graciously accepted my offer of personal bodyguard to Alice.

"I'll be over later tonight." I called after them as they left my office, then turned to my Beta. "What?"

Bret shook his head with a faint smile. "You're living in the dog-house, my friend."

"What is that supposed to mean?"

"It is clear that the Hunter doesn't want protection; she wants to prove that she can manage things on her own."

"I know she can." I countered. "I just want to ensure I'm there if things go sideways."

"She doesn't see it that way."

"I would like you to watch Alice during the day." I countered.

Again, Bret showed a faint, too-knowing smile. "I'll handle the paperwork from the attack at the Thorpe's house. You should go home and rest a bit before you take up bodyguard duty tonight."

"I'll get to that."

I tried calling Roman again. I can't imagine why Roman is not picking up my calls. After that failed attempt, I went to Hugh to update him on what I'd learned in the past few hours since last speaking to him. But, of course, I kept Charlie's identification a secret, along with any information about the Hunter Society.

Hugh was not happy over me insisting on protecting Alice. I almost had to threaten him with my resignation, but Hugh relented. He agreed that if a vampire is the killer, then ordinary officers — those who know nothing about the supernatural — won't be enough to protect Alice when he decides to attack again.

My next stop before heading home is to talk to Baxter. I hope he's had enough rest because the task I have for him will be tedious. I found him at his desk, eager to help, when I stopped beside him. I tasked him with looking into global crimes similar to ours, explaining that I was curious if we were dealing with a copycat killer. I hope to learn which Hunter families have been attacked and who might be next.

Finally getting to my flat, I was able to catch about four hours of sleep before making my way over to the Thorpe house. Mrs. Thorpe greeted me warmly when I entered their home while Mr. Thorpe narrowed a suspicious gaze on me. Automatically I looked for Alice but didn't see her. Smiling politely, I apologized for the intrusion into their home. Mrs. Thorpe waved off my apology, far too thrilled to have me protecting her daughter. Mr. Thorpe said he wished to speak privately and ushered me upstairs to his study.

"What is the Alpha of Stellacote doing offering his time to protect my daughter, a Hunter?"

"What do you know of Hunters disappearing?" I countered as we took seats.

Mr. Thorpe frowned. "Don't change the subject."

"I'm not." I half lied. "The vampire that attacked Miss Thorpe has also attacked the Hunter family in Australia, and they've gone missing. So, it knows Miss Thorpe is a Hunter and will come after her again."

"So, you offered protection to stop the vampire?"

"Yes."

"And what of my daughter?"

I shifted uncomfortably under his gaze. He knows. He must know. Knows that Alice and I have met on multiple occasions. Knows we've kissed. I tried not to show any emotion on my face beyond my duty as a detective to catch a killer. His steady dark brown gaze penetrating, I could only imagine what this man was like when he was a younger, more active Hunter. It made me edgy and uncomfortable. Even my wolf backed away a step as if it wanted to keep its distance from this man.

"I don't understand."

"Did you only offer to protect Alice to stop the vampire?" Mr. Thorpe stared me down. "Or do you truly want to protect my daughter?"

"Yes." I cleared my throat, trying not to show the older Hunter how intimidating he could be. "I want to protect Alice — with my life if I have to. I know I have no right to make such a claim. I also know she'll do whatever it takes to take down the vampire that attacked her. She shouldn't have to do it alone."

Mr. Thorpe was silent for a short while, considering me. "I only recently found out that the leaders of the Hunter Society are disappearing. First, the family in Japan disappeared, then in France, followed by Australia. The Hunters remaining have gone into survival mode, and their communication is limited. All I know is that it was a massively coordinated attack and that someone within the Hunter Society has betrayed us."

"Do you have any idea who could have betrayed all of you?"

"No."

"Father?"

We both fell silent and turned to the door. Alice knocked as she opened it. Her eyes widened at the sight of me then she glared at me before focusing on her father. She's still upset with me. But, eventually, she will get over her stubbornness. When she does, she'll realize that my protection is what's best for her.

"A letter came for you." She announced.

"From who?" Mr. Thorpe stood, taking the cream envelope from her.

"There's no return address."

I watched the envelope exchange hands, Mr. Thorpe's name scrawled across the front and sealed with a bright red wax seal. Mr. Thorpe frowned, looking at it. He opened it, read it, then handed it over to me. Inside there was a card with the words: *you're next*. I paled. I am not going to let the vampire take Alice. I tried calling Roman again. If I can't get ahold of the wolf soon, I'll have to fly to Europe and see him personally.

Mr. Thorpe forced a smile toward Alice. "Thank you, sweetie."

"Is it important?" She eyed the envelope in my hands. "It has the Hunter symbol on the back."

"It's not the news I was hoping to hear." His response was evasive. "You said you are planning on visiting Queen tonight?"

"I am. It's unlike her to let a vampire roam this city unchecked."

"Why don't you go grab some weapons? Queen's house might be on edge. It'll be best to arrive prepared."

She nodded, pushing a grandfather clock out of the way and slipping behind it. Once the clock was back in place, Mr. Thorpe turned his attention back to me.

"Don't let that vampire harm my daughter. Whatever is going on, she should not be dragged into this."

"I promise to protect her Mr. Thorpe."

The man eyed me as if judging my sincerity. "Call me Jeffery."

# CHAPTER SIX

## ALICE

MOTHER EXCITEDLY WENT IN search of my father. I assumed to tell him about all the protection the Stellacote police would provide. I went in search of ibuprofen. I could hear my mother's pleased tone as she spoke, her voice drifting from the sunroom.

I wasn't quite sure what to do with myself right now. I looked up the stairs. With my back still sore, training isn't too appealing right now. I want to go out and search for the vampire, but I should probably talk to Queen first. Pulling out my phone, I texted Josie Walker, my daytime contact for Queen Ana, informing her that I'll be visiting tonight. Then I quickly sent a second one to add that a bodyguard would accompany me.

I hate this lull. This in-between time when something needs to be done, but there's no clear path to move forward. It makes me antsy. I hate not doing anything. With a resigned sigh, I marched out the patio door to our backyard. Staying all cooped up inside is the last thing I want to do right now. Maybe some fresh air will help clear my mind to the next step.

Years ago, my father built a rose maze just for my mother. Roses are her favourite flower. They used to take walks in the labyrinth when they wanted to be alone. The labyrinth was my favourite hiding spot. I'm sure my father knew where to find me, but it was my mother who always came. She'd sit beside me, waiting for me to start talking about whatever issue I had that urged me to hide. I frowned at the memory. Mother and I used to be close, but it's been over five years since we've been able to talk like best friends.

"Your mother tells me Detective Lune offered to be your bodyguard."

I turned at the sound of my father's voice from behind me. "He did."

"Why?"

I shrugged. I don't want to think about his reason. Almost certain it's because I'm a weak human. So instead, I informed him of my plans.

"We're going to see Queen tonight."

My father narrowed his eyes at me. "You know you can't just barge in on her."

"I've informed Josie. Besides, Queen has never turned me away."

"You said we, so the detective is going with you?"

"Yes, Father."

He sighed, pulling me into a gentle hug. "Be safe in your hunt."

He let me go with a kiss on the top of my head. I turned back to the maze that took over most of the backyard. I had long ago memorized the way to the center where I could rest in the gazebo in peace. The scent of roses overpowered all other scents as I manoeuvred through the maze. Another memory came to me the deeper I ventured.

Sometimes, late at night, when my parents thought I was sound asleep, soft music would wake me. I'd peer out my balcony to see my parents dancing in the maze's center.

Reaching the center, I went straight for the gazebo and lay down on the cool marble bench — a balm to the pain in my back. I closed my eyes, a gentle breeze passing over my skin as I relaxed. Since returning home, I've found this maze to be my haven, my freedom spot during the day. It's where I can get away from my mother's overprotective ways. Since her mental breakdowns, it's rare for her to leave the house; if she does, it's only for a short time. So, this house is her safe haven.

My mind wandered, soft music began playing in my head, and I pictured myself dancing with Ryan just like my parents used to. The image brought a smile to my lips. His hand gently caressed my back as he held me close, gazing down at me with his brown eyes. I felt calm and protected in his hold. Then the image contorted, and Ryan was replaced with the blond vampire. I struggled to push away, but his grip tightened as he held me close.

"What a wonderful scene Hunter." He smiled, the sight of his fangs sending a shiver through me.

"This isn't real." I tried pushing away harder and shaking my head. "It's all in my head."

"Of course, it's all in your head." His hand was firm on my back. "A place where only I can go."

"What do you mean?" I tilted my head back to see him. His blue eyes danced.

He leaned in, and his fangs brushed along my neck. "Tell me your name, Hunter."

I stiffened. Queen has always warned me that names hold power for vampires. There's no way I will give this vampire power over me.

"No."

"A name for a name."

"You first." I taunted.

He brought his lips to my ear, voice so low I had to strain to hear him. "Carden."

"Alice." My name slipped out unwillingly, and he smiled.

"You can not hide from me Alice. I will see you again." With that, he bit down on my neck.

I jolted up, eyes wide as I felt for my neck. I cursed at the nightmare my mind conjured. Glancing around, I noted the sun was casting orange tones, indicating I was outside for longer than anticipated. I made my way back inside. Sitting on the small table near the front door sat an envelope with my father's name on it. Picking it up, I turned it around to see it sealed with the Hunter symbol. I rushed upstairs to my father's study.

"Father?" I opened the door, surprised to see Ryan, remembering why he was there and glared at him. "A letter came for you."

"From who?" My father took the offered envelope.

"There's no return address." I handed it to him with the seal facing up.

I wanted to ask what the message inside read, but the words froze on my tongue. As my father read the note, his jaw tightened. He passed the envelope to Ryan, who paled briefly after reading the note before anger and determination filled his features. Whatever was inside could not be good by their reactions. Now I really want to know. Unfortunately, Ryan slipped the message back into the envelope before I could peek. Ryan tried calling someone as my father forced a smile.

"Thank you, sweetie."

"Is it important?" I eyed the envelope, curious and itching to read it. "It has the Hunter symbol on the back."

"It's not the news I was hoping to hear." My father responded evasively. "You said you were planning on visiting Queen tonight?"

"I am." I answered slowly. He was changing the subject. "It's not like her to let a vampire roam this city unchecked."

"Why don't you go grab some weapons? Queen's house might be on edge, and it'll be best to stay on your toes."

I nodded, moving over to the grandfather clock. I had never seen my father scared before — and whatever was inside that envelope frightened him. As I descended the spiralling stairs, I pondered what, or who, on this Earth could cause that reaction.

Stopping in front of the weapons table, I stared down at them, not truly seeing what lay before me. I reconsidered not going after this vampire after seeing my father's fear and Ryan's range of emotions. Irritated with myself for even considering backing down, I shook my head, focusing on the table. I added sheaths to my arms, but after a quick review, I decided not to wear them. It would be disrespectful to Queen. Then I thought of Carden and changed my mind. I'll have to change my top to cover them. Finally, I added a belt that doubles as a whip and my favourite necklace — a leaf that folds out to reveal a short blade.

I prefer to attach more weapons in case Carden tries anything outside of mind tricks but know both my mother and Queen would not appreciate it. Resigning myself to the few weapons I currently wore, I returned upstairs. My father and Ryan were no longer in the study. I quickly glanced to verify that the door was closed. Now is my chance to look for that envelope. I lifted papers on the desk, opened drawers, and even looked in the garbage. I groaned at what I'd found. In the trash lay ashes and the remnants of the red wax. Now I'll never know what scared my father. Disappointed, I ventured to my room to change into a long-sleeve off-shoulder top to cover my weapons.

Opening my door, Lynol lowered his hand, primed to knock, and informed me dinner was ready. I followed him down to the dining room. Stopping in the doorway at the horrible sight within. Lucas and my mother chatted pleasantly as they sat across each other, an empty place setting for me beside Lucas. Ryan sat at the end of the long table, as far from them as possible. My father didn't seem too pleased with the setup either.

"Alice." Ryan whispered, drawing my attention to him, and I noted that he held a steak knife tightly in his grip. "It's early, but we can go to Queen's now."

I frowned, a hand on my stomach as it growled. "I haven't eaten all day."

"When you're ready to leave." He let the sentence fall.

"Alice!" My mother announced brightly. "Stop bothering the detective and come sit."

"Alice." My name came as a sigh on Lucas's lips as I forced myself to sit at my spot. "I'm so glad to see you well. I was so worried."

"Isn't that sweet?" My mother cooed. "Lucas came to check on you, so I invited him to stay for dinner."

"Who told you I was home?" I raised a questioning brow. I certainly didn't.

"No one." He responded with a shrug and a slight glare toward Ryan. "I came to check on your parents too."

I bit my tongue at the rude comment I wanted to throw at him when my mother swooned over his kindness. My father scowled. Soup, the first meal on the menu, came out of the kitchen. The food gave me an excuse not to talk to Lucas. My mother took up the role of gracious host by monopolizing the dinner conversation with Lucas. He turned on the charm, and it truly set in that my mother is too easily manipulated. I glanced at my father, and he looked at my mother worriedly. The soup was replaced with beef tenderloin. I was grateful. It gave me an excuse to grab the steak knife.

"Lucas." My father finally spoke, taking hold of my wrist. "What are your intentions here?"

Lucas flushed. "My intentions?"

"It's a simple question."

Determination settled on his features. He pushed his chair away, getting down on one knee and taking my free hand. "Alice Thorpe, will you marry me?"

My mother gasped, fanning herself. I swear there was a growl from the other end of the table. I gaped at Lucas, momentarily blindsided by the question. Then anger filled me. As my hand tightened around the knife, so did my father's grip on my wrist. I'm confident I've already turned him down once. Though last time he didn't ask me to marry him.

"Did you say marriage?" I questioned to make sure I heard him right.

"I did."

"Give the poor boy an answer." My mother scolded me when I took too long.

"Was I not clear the other night?" I pulled my hand away from him and stood. "No, I will not marry you."

Ryan came up beside me, offering his hand. "Shall we?"

"Thank you." I whispered, taking his hand.

"Where are you taking my daughter, detective?" My mother questioned harshly.

"It is fine Vivian." My father soothed. "I asked them to run an errand for me."

"But Jeffery." She bit her lower lip. "The attacker."

"Ryan won't let anyone harm Alice."

I heard nothing else my parents might have said as we were already out the door. Ryan had parked his car off to the side in a parking spot reserved for short-term guests. He opened the passenger door for me. I still felt horrified and sick over Lucas's proposal.

"Maybe I hit him too hard." I commented out loud.

"Excuse me?" Ryan glanced at me, brow raised.

"At the party, when he forced a kiss on me, I hit him in the head with a triangle from the pool table."

His lips quirked at my explanation.

"I don't want anything to do with him."

"You can always file a restraining order. I'd be more than happy to put it into effect."

I laughed. "Thank you Ryan. I'll consider it."

We fell silent. Eventually, Ryan pulled up to Queen's residence. I led the way up to the doors feeling better now that Lucas wasn't around. Josie and Joel greeted us in the entryway. Joel's usually irritated gaze slid past me to Ryan, his eyes narrowing. Even Josie raised a questioning brow.

"I did say I was bringing my bodyguard." I reminded them.

"You didn't say it was the Alpha." Josie countered.

"No, I did not."

"Queen won't be happy you tricked her." A faint smile curved Joel's lip.

He's never liked me, and the reason, Josie told me, is because I'm a Hunter. Hunters killed their parents when they were tracking down some supernatural — wrong place, wrong time — it left them orphaned, and Queen took them in instantly. It's left him hating anyone with the title of Hunter, not just the ones who killed their parents by mistake. So, when I learnt of their tragedy, I looked into it. The Hunters who killed their parents were stripped of their status and killed by revenging wolves the following year. None of that information would appease Joel — his parents are still dead.

"Best to leave now before you feel her wrath." Joel taunted.

"I didn't trick her. I only neglected to state exactly who I was bringing." I smiled broadly. "You didn't think to call me to ask about the bodyguard."

"Enough." Queen's voice echoed around the entryway. "Bring the young Hunter and the Alpha to me."

Joel scowled, turning on his heels and leading us to the sitting room. Queen Ana lounged comfortably on a chaise with a glass of what I assumed was blood. Even in casual clothing, Queen still looks regal. I would never admit to my father that I've been visiting Queen over the years to learn about vampire politics and their history to better myself as a Hunter. During that time, I've grown to respect the vampire. Hunters aren't supposed to get as close to the vampire and wolf leaders as I have. I find it an old way of thinking. My father might appear to like Ryan, but Queen is a different story.

"Young Hunter." Queen's voice brought me out of my head. "Why did you bring the Alpha into my home?"

"Queen." I bowed respectfully. "Detective Lune is my bodyguard."

"So, he is here on official business?"

"He is."

"Very well." She sat up, gesturing to the chairs before her. "Sit and explain to me what you came here to say."

"You should already know." Ryan glared.

I sat, looking up at Ryan, waiting for him to do the same. He scowled, reluctantly taking the other chair. He sat on the edge, poised to stand or lunge. I leaned back comfortably and accepted the water offered by one of the many vampires living in the house.

"You came armed." Queen noted, ignoring Ryan's earlier statement. "You've never once come armed before."

"How many times have you been here?" Ryan growled the question at me.

"Many times, Alpha." Queen smiled. "Has the young Hunter never been in your house?"

"I'm a Hunter. Of course, I've been here to speak with Queen about vampire matters." I replied defensively. "Queen, I'd appreciate it if you don't toy with Ryan."

"My apologies young Hunter. Tell me, why are you in need of a bodyguard?"

"I'm sure you've heard of the attacks in Capital Hill." I didn't wait for a response. "A single vampire has committed those attacks. So many innocent lives have been taken."

"I've heard the rumours."

"They aren't rumours." Ryan countered.

"None of the vampires under me are the culprit you seek." Queen stated.

I pursed my lips. "The vampire from those attacks also attacked me, sinking his fangs into my neck. Ryan purified me and is now my bodyguard, as we suspect this vampire will come for me again."

I observed Queen's expression carefully. Fear flashed across the vampire's face so quickly that I would have missed it if I had blinked. I wasn't feeling as confident anymore; first, my father, then Ryan, and now Queen have all displayed fear. Something is happening in Stellacote, and no one wants me to be involved. As much as I want to prove to Ryan that I'm not a weak human, I'm beginning to doubt it is even possible.

Queen masked her features. "As I've said, none of the vampires under me are the culprit you seek."

"I doubt that." Ryan grumbled.

"If I could help, I would." She glared at him. "I would have sent out my Sanguis to deal with the problem."

"There is something you could help with." I interrupted whatever Ryan was going to say. "Perhaps you can send your Sanguis to search for the blue-eyed golden-blond-haired vampire. I'm sure you understand that as a detective, Ryan must track down the killer of Capital Hill, and as a Hunter, I must take care of this vampire. Car-." The name stuck in my throat as if I was being choked. "This vampire can not be allowed to cause more trouble in our city."

"I understand." Queen answered sharply. "You may show yourselves out now."

"Wait a minute!" Ryan jumped up, intending to follow Queen out of the room, but I stood to block him. "Out of my way Alice!"

"We've been asked to leave."

Ryan stared down at me for a heartbeat. "Fine."

I smiled faintly, again taking the lead out. I didn't dare speak until we were safe in the car and driving away. "She's scared."

"Who is?"

"Queen Ana." I shifted in my seat to face him. "She's scared of Car-." I frowned, hating how I couldn't say his name out loud. "This vampire."

"I doubt that." He scoffed.

"She even said the vampire is not one of hers. If she's scared, then he must be stronger than her."

Ryan glanced at me. "Are you sure?"

"I'm sure. I saw her fear. It was brief, but it was there." I frowned, returning to a forward position. "How am I supposed to take care of a vampire that even has Queen scared?"

"Hey." Ryan reached over, taking my hand. "Don't be doubting yourself now. You're an excellent Hunter."

I blushed at the compliment but couldn't bring myself to believe him. I still can't defeat my father in our training sessions, and I doubt I could beat Queen in a sparring match. Queen and her Sanguis have always taken care of troublesome vampires. I have never needed to go after one before now. As for the wolves I've taken down, I've been lucky they were young and didn't know how to fight correctly yet. My doubt in my abilities grew during the car ride. I may be a Hunter for Stellacote, but I'm not a full-fledged Hunter in the eyes of the Hunter Society. I don't know what to do about Carden.

# CHAPTER SEVEN

## RYAN

I COULD SENSE ALICE'S growing unease in her silence. I don't know how to help her. We swung by a fast-food restaurant before returning to her house since she didn't eat much at supper time. She nibbled on the food while I drove around, not wanting to take her back immediately. I want to know what is going through her mind, but she refuses to speak or even look at me.

When I finally drove her home, the car was barely put in park before she got out without a word. I pulled the keys out of the ignition and locked the car before turning to look at the Thorpe house. Alice was already at the front door. She hesitated on going in, looking back at me briefly before entering. I followed. My phone rang just as my foot hit the bottom step.

"Detective Lune." I answered automatically without looking at the caller ID.

"Did you see the news?" Bret asked. "Probably not, or else you would have called me earlier."

I froze. "I would have called about what?"

"News channels got wind of the Capital Hill murders."

"They what?" I roared into the phone.

"Captain Forest and I have handled it." Bret spoke over me.

"Handled it how?"

"The moment we saw the news, we tried to reach you." He explained. "When we couldn't reach you, we contacted each other. Captain Forest and I tore the office apart to find multiple bugs. Someone has been listening in on our case."

"Where exactly? How long have they been there?"

"We found them in various locations. Who knows how long they've been there." Bret answered calmly. "Captain held a press conference to help calm the mess and is personally looking into those bugs. How are things on your end?"

I looked up at the Thorpe house. "Jeffery received a threat saying he's next, or maybe it was meant for Alice. We're not sure, but it came with the Hunter symbol. Lucas stopped by to propose to Alice. Oh, and we went to visit Queen."

"How did that go?"

"Alice believes she's afraid of this vampire. I'm finding that hard to believe."

"Interesting." Bret paused, seeming to be in thought.

"What is exactly?"

"Oh, nothing."

There was an amused note to his tone. I frowned.

"Bret." I warned.

"How are you holding up with Lucas's proposal?"

I growled my response. "She said no, and he's still alive."

Bret laughed. "Good."

"Did you expect me to tell you he's in the hospital?"

Bret's laughter died down. "You have more control than that. So, what's the next step in tracking this vampire?"

I ran a hand over my face as I refocused my thoughts. "Get me a flight out to Europe. Last I checked, Roman is still in France. That Alpha hasn't called me back, so I'm going to him. I want you to watch over Alice while I'm gone."

"Did something happen that you're concerned about?"

"I fear without a clue to who or where this vampire is —." I trailed off, afraid to verbally announce my concerns over Alice's current state or even consider what she'd do to pull the vampire from hiding. "Just watch her."

"Very well. I'll hand you your flight details in the morning."

At the end of the conversation, I entered the Thorpe house. Jeffery was waiting for me in the entryway. First, he inquired about the trip to Queen. I told him the little information I gathered and Alice's belief. Jeffery didn't appear pleased by that piece of news and even less pleased when he asked about the Capital Hill murders that broke out on the news channels. I cringed and told him about the conversation I had just had with Bret.

"Do you think the vampire did all that just to cause a panic?"

I didn't consider the possibility. "I'm not sure. With everything that's been happening, I can say for certain that the vampire will come for Alice soon. Along with both you and your wife."

"I'll dust off my Hunter skills to protect my family."

"I doubt you'd let your skills get rusty." I commented lightly.

Jeffery smiled dangerously. "Just keep that in mind if something happens to my daughter."

I froze, a sudden jolt of fear running through me at the subtle threat. That salt and pepper hair is deceiving. Most supernatural would be lowering their guard around this man, thinking he's old and weak. I know better than to assume someone's strength based on their looks. He could probably still be a workth opponent. I watched the older Hunter go upstairs before I turned to lock the front door. I did an entire tour of the main floor, ensuring all windows and doors were locked. Then I did the same upstairs in all but the main bedroom. I am positive that Jeffery would have done that himself. My last stop was Alice's room.

I frowned at the soft night breeze that hit me as I silently entered her room. The doors to her balcony were gone, and flimsy pieces of wood boarded the opening, leaving Alice completely vulnerable. Those should have been entirely fixed by now. My eyes then drifted over to my Hunter. She slept with a pained expression. Closing the door quietly behind me, I went over to her. I gently touched her shoulder, whispering her name. Alice woke up, eyes wide and unfocused. She knocked my hand away and tackled me to the ground with a dagger pressed against my throat. Her long brown hair fell forward, framing her face and tickling mine as she hovered over me.

"Alice." I called more firmly yet softly to not arouse her father's attention. "You're safe."

"Ryan?" She blinked down at me, eyes coming into focus. "I could have killed you."

"Maybe." I admitted. "Maybe not."

She could have injured me if she wasn't half asleep. Alice removed the dagger from my throat but kept it tight in her hand. I stayed on my back, placing my hands gently on her thighs. I needed to touch her.

71

"What are you doing in my room?"

"Making sure the house is locked. I came here last."

She looked at the damaged balcony doors. "That might be a little difficult."

I studied her face. "Were you having a bad dream?"

Fear flooded Alice's features. "He was calling for me."

"What?"

I sat up so suddenly that Alice squeaked as she slid from her spot on my chest to my lap. My hands slid up to her waist, keeping her in an upward position when I moved.

"How is that possible? I cleaned the bite."

"I don't know." My shirt muffled her voice as she buried her face in my chest and wrapped her arms around me. "I don't know if I'm strong enough to face him."

"You are strong enough." I wrapped my arms around her, just holding her against me. "I won't let you face him alone."

Despite Alice's bravado during the day, I knew she had to be scared. I didn't realize how frightened she truly was. Or maybe the vampire calling her brought on this fear. We stayed like that for a long time. When Alice's tense body finally relaxed, I lifted her, carrying her to her bed. When I laid her down, I took a step back. Alice reached out, taking my hand before I moved too far away.

"Don't go." She pleaded. Her voice was soft and vulnerable.

"I won't."

I wanted to run around the property, but the pleading look in her eyes had me sitting down, my back against the bed. Alice slid off the bed, curling herself in my lap. Sighing, I pulled the sheet off the bed and tucked it around us. I held her in my arms. She sighed against me, relaxing fully. Alice's breathing evened out. She'd fallen asleep, a peaceful expression on her features this time. I rested my chin on her head, finding pleasure and peace with her in my arms as sleep took me over as well.

# CHAPTER EIGHT

## ALICE

I woke cradled in warmth. Snuggling deeper into that feeling, I didn't want to open my eyes.

"Mmm, Ryan." I sighed contently.

"Morning Alice."

His deep rumble had my eyes shooting open. Initially, I wasn't sure what I saw, but then it hit me. Pushing back, I realized I was cradled in Ryan's arms. I'd fallen asleep against him and never moved. He never moved me. His heart kept a steady beat under my hand as he held me. Horror and embarrassment crept up my cheeks. I could feel them getting warmer and pushed further away. Ryan's grip on me tightened, stopping me from escaping.

"You're still here." I gave up trying to escape.

He frowned at me. "You asked me not to go."

"Well." I squirmed in his lap. "I thought you'd leave after I fell asleep. I didn't think you'd stay the whole night."

"Don't do that." He growled, his eyes closing as if he were in pain.

"I'm sorry?"

"Don't squirm."

I stopped. Ryan opened his eyes to look down at me. They were glowing, bright yellow peeking through the brown. His wolf sat right on the edge. I sucked in a breath, and my heart sped up — not out of fear. Ryan could never scare me. Keeping eye contact, I reached up and pulled his head down for a kiss. His grip on me tightened even more, and he kissed me like a hungry animal. The need he kissed me with sent little tendrils of excitement through me.

"Alice." He pulled back for air. "We need to stop."

"Why?" I questioned, brushing my lips against his, desperate for his back on mine.

"Because I have a flight out to France today."

I blinked at him. "What?"

"I'm going to meet the Alpha out there."

"How long are you going to be gone?"

"For as little time as possible."

I pushed myself back. This time he let me. I scrambled off Ryan's lap. I shouldn't have let him get close. I'm just a weak human, not strong enough to handle him. That's probably what he thinks. Hunter or not, he's still the Alpha of Stellacote. Before this moment, we were good. We worked well together when we focused on tracking down monsters.

I ran my hands through my hair. I needed a moment to settle my heart and hide my hurt. Then, when I felt like I was ready, I turned back to Ryan.

"Okay. So, you're going to France."

Ryan watched me, remaining on the floor. "Bret will be here. He will keep you safe while I'm gone."

"How long has this been planned?"

"Since last night."

"Were you going to tell me you were leaving?" I don't want him to hear my hurt, but I can't seem to keep it out of my tone. "Or were you planning on just slipping out now that it's Bret's turn to babysit me?"

Ryan let out an exasperated sound. "You don't need a babysitter. You're perfectly capable of protecting yourself."

"Am I now?" I countered, crossing my arms. "Then I don't need you or Bret around if I'm perfectly capable of protecting myself."

"Not against this vampire." He glared, his shoulders tensing. "He's far more dangerous than anything you've ever faced before. You need the backup."

"Yet my backup is going to France." I turned to my closet, collected clothes then stormed off to my bathroom. "Goodbye, safe travels detective."

"Alice." Ryan called out as I slammed the door shut.

I re-opened the door. "Maybe when you get back, I'll be married to Lucas. Heaven knows my mother will push for it."

I know he doesn't deserve the terrible lie, but I'm feeling hurt by his leaving. For all I know, this vampire will attack me while he's gone. Fury filled Ryan's face. He stood, and in a few long, determined strides, he was at the bathroom door. He pushed the door open wider, cupped my face in his large hands and kissed me. I felt my knees go weak at the possessiveness he portrayed in the act.

"You are mine Alice." He declared with a subtle growl to his tone.

"You are leaving, Ryan."

He kissed me again. "You are mine Alice. When this vampire is taken care of, I will make you mine."

I shivered. "How?"

"Every way a man can."

I curled my fingers in his shirt. "Why can't I go with you?"

Ryan gave my lips a quick peck and wrapped his hands around my own. "Who will protect Stellacote?"

"Bret." I answered without hesitation.

He chuckled. "I'd love for you to come along."

"But?"

"The Alpha in France is just as dangerous as this vampire." He brought my hands up to his lips, kissing the knuckles. "The only difference is that I know this danger. I know how to handle him."

I pouted. "Just go."

"Alice."

"The sooner you leave, the sooner you can come back."

His shoulders relaxed as a smile curved his lips. One final quick kiss, and he turned to leave. I watched him leave my bedroom, and then I closed the door to the bathroom. I took a long hot shower. Before donning my bra, I examined my back in the mirror. It showed a deep purple bruise covering a good portion of my back. It also hurt like hell to get the bra on and the t-shirt over my head.

Once dressed, I brushed my teeth and ran a brush through my hair. Then, I rushed back to my room to pick up my ringing phone.

"Hello?"

"Alice." Josie replied in a mere whisper.

"Josie. What's wrong?"

"Can you meet me today?"

"Of course." I told her. "When and where?"

"Carnival Mall, the food court at noon."

"I'll be there."

There was a sigh of relief. Then she spoke louder. "Of course. I'll inform Queen the moment she's available."

With that, Josie hung up on me. I could only suspect someone was walking by, and she wanted to cover up why she was on the phone. It's rare for Josie to be calling me. Whatever the reason, it has to be important. For her to want to meet outside of Queen's home, well, that just made me suspiciously curious. I called up my friend Patty asking if she wanted to go to the mall with me. I need a cover to go there. It would seem odd to my family and Bret if I only went for lunch and then returned home. So, I planned to pick her up in half an hour, just enough time to grab a bite to eat before heading out.

I made my way down to the kitchen. My father was there serving Bret coffee. He greeted me with a kiss on the forehead and poured me a cup as well. He returned to his seat when my mother came into the kitchen. She headed straight for the coffee pot.

She poured herself a cup. Added sugar and cream, then took a gulp. She carefully placed the cup on the island countertop and glared at me. My father wrapped an arm around her waist and kissed her cheek. I ignored the look from my mother. Instead, I turned to the toaster to insert an English muffin.

"You were quite rude to Lucas last night." My mother finally stated.

"How was I rude?" I countered while keeping my back to her.

"You didn't give Lucas a chance to explain how much he wants you, how well he'll treat you as his wife. Instead, you ran away with that detective."

"Mother, I don't even know Lucas." I turned, crossing my arms, ignoring her disgust when she mentioned Ryan. "Why would I marry him?"

My mother smiled as if she'd won a prize. "I thought that was the case, so I arranged for the two of you to have dinner tonight."

"No. Absolutely not."

"How else are you supposed to get to know him?"

"I don't want to get to know him." I glanced to my father for help. "You can't force me to go on a date with someone."

My mother pouted. "But you two were getting along so well at the party."

"We did have a pleasant conversation." I agreed. "But I realized during that conversation that we are not compatible. I don't want anything to do with Lucas."

"I won't cancel the reservations. He'll be here at four thirty to pick you up."

"Was there anyone else at the party that your mother should know about?" My father interjected.

My English muffin popped. I turned to add butter and jam to my breakfast. My mother gasped.

"Who?" She demanded. "And why didn't you tell me about him before? I must meet him."

"Mother." I groaned. "Let me handle my own love life. I appreciate your efforts but refuse to be rushed into a marriage."

"Fine. But you're still going to dinner with Lucas. He's a sweet boy."

With that final statement, she picked up her coffee and left the kitchen. With a shake of his head, my father followed her. I stuffed the English muffin in my mouth. Bret had sat on a stool and stayed silent while the scene unfurled itself. I only glared at the man, unwarranted, but my mother always seemed to set me off. Or maybe it's because of the forced dinner with Lucas. There was a concerned look in his eyes.

"What?"

"Is your mother okay?" He asked gently.

I looked in the direction she'd disappeared in. "Not really."

"Are you going to be okay?"

"I will be."

He watched me silently for a moment. "What do you plan to do today?"

"Carnival Mall." I sighed. Thankful he was changing the subject. "I'm to be picking up a friend soon."

"Very well." He nodded. "When exactly are we leaving?"

"We?" I raised a brow at him.

"I'm driving you Miss Thorpe." He responded nonchalantly. "Losing you in the mall parking lot would be too easy."

"Well, we can leave now, I guess."

I gave him the other half of my English muffin, suddenly not hungry. He picked it up and turned to lead me to the front door. He chauffeured me to Patty's house with my directions.

Patricia "Patty" Russel has been my best friend for years. We met on prom night. I happened to be wandering when I heard a shrill scream and went to investigate. I found Patty fighting off the advances of a persistent guy. I stepped in, knocking him down with a single punch. Shocked and grateful, Patty treated my hand, and we talked and became instant friends.

Patty is now a registered nurse with a Master's degree after eight years of schooling. During that time, I became her practice subject, especially with the injuries I received while hunting. I claim I'm helping women against abusive men, which is how I get so banged up and bruised. Though I never go to Patty if a supernatural left a mark that would raise questions — such as claw marks along my arms. My father handles those injuries. The Hunter Society's unique healing balm also helps — no blemish remains on my body.

"Hey." I greeted as Patty slid into the back seat of Bret's car with me. "I'm so glad you had today off."

Patty smiled. "Working as a nurse for the rich has its perks! So, why call me for a sudden trip to the mall?"

I groaned, leaning my head back on the seat. "My mother is doing a match-making thing with someone named Lucas."

"Start from the beginning." She ordered.

"You know about the party my mother threw the other night." I began. "That's when I met Lucas. He seemed nice, better than the other suitors there. Mother walked in when we were having a civil conversation. Tonight, she's set up a dinner with him for tonight."

"What are you leaving out?"

My lips twitched. "I hit him on the head when he forced a kiss on me."

"Not hard enough." Patty grimaced. "Especially if he agreed to this dinner."

"There's no doubt he jumped at the opportunity."

"You know what you have to do?"

"No." I replied cautiously. "But you're going to tell me."

"Tell your mother about Ryan."

"That's a little complicated."

Patty frowned. "Don't tell me he's married."

"He's not married." I assured her. "Ryan is single."

"Then what's complicated?" Her blue eyes glittered mischievously. "From what you've told me, it sounds like he likes you as much as you like him."

I glanced at Bret through the rear-view mirror. He was smiling but kept his eyes on the road, trying to pretend he wasn't listening. I'm pretty sure whatever I said in this car to Patty, he'll keep to himself.

Returning my focus to Patty, I elaborated. "Ryan is a detective. His job can be dangerous, and his hours aren't exactly steady. But, if my mother has her way, I will marry some social elite who will keep me safe in the confines of Capital Hill. That will be as far as my mother will let me go."

"You've said your mother has mental health issues, but that's ridiculous. You can't keep agreeing to your mother's wants just because she can relapse and break down again." Patty scolded. "It's not fair to you."

"I can't do that to my father. He looked so run down the first time, and I had never seen him in that state before."

"Alice, you have to think of yourself. As long as I've known you, you've gone after what you wanted. That includes sneaking out of your house to meet up with Ryan. So why are you now backing away from what you want?"

"I'm afraid what I want this time will do more than send my mother into a relapse. I'm afraid of how much I want Ryan."

"Miss Thorpe." Bret interrupted. "We're at the mall."

I looked out the window to see he had parked. Stellacote's Carnival Mall is the main attraction for the city. Five floors of shopping with a mini amusement park inside. Attractions such as a carousel, laser tag, rock climbing, and more added to the fun of shopping for all ages. Getting out of the car, Bret promised to keep his distance — we exchanged phone numbers to contact each other in an emergency.

Patty looped an arm through mine. She questioned me about Bret, assuming he was just a chauffeur. I explained that Bret is my bodyguard while Ryan is away trying to learn more about a case he's working on. At least, I'm assuming that's why he suddenly left for France. Patty quickly guessed it was about the Capital Hill Killer she'd heard about on the news, then pointed out that Ryan wouldn't have a bodyguard on me if he weren't worried for my safety.

I chose not to tell Patty that I'd already been attacked. Today's mall trip is a cover for meeting with Josie. It'll also be an excellent opportunity to do something normal. Telling Patty the truth about anything would worry her, and our time at the mall wouldn't be fun.

We began on the bottom floor. It took about an hour to walk around each floor. I mostly window shopped, only entering the stores when Patty saw something she wanted to try on. Patty carried a few bags by the third floor, and we were hungry. So I suggested we stop for food. My meeting time with Josie will be shortly. Unfortunately, this morning's coffee and half of an English muffin wasn't enough food to keep me going. Shopping with Patty can be a marathon.

The mall's food court is on the third floor, ideally situated in the middle. There are a variety of options to choose from. With a quick scan of the food court, I settled on Thai. Patty joined me in line. After ordering, we took our food to one of the few free tables that were filling up fast. Partway through our meal, I received a text from Josie.

"I'm going to run to the washroom." I announced, leaving my friend and slipping down the hallway to the washrooms. Josie waited for me by the baby changing room. "Okay, I'm here."

Josie pulled me into the room. Closing the door, she then spoke in a whisper. "Queen, she's in danger."

I frowned. "In danger? What do you mean?"

"I overheard some Sanguis talking about taking out the Hunters, and then they plan to overthrow Queen."

"Did you tell Queen?"

"I did." Josie gripped my arms. "She waved it off like it was nothing. But, Alice, you have to do something."

"Josie." I took hold of her elbows. "I'm sorry, but I can't do anything. Vampire politics are not something the Hunter Society will step into. As for the threat on the Hunters, I need proof. Right now, the society will think Queen sent you to tell me all this to start a war."

"She wouldn't do that!"

"I know that." I assuaged her. "Did you hear anything that will allow me to look into the threat?"

She nodded. "I heard something about Jack's tonight at seven. I think it's a place."

"Okay." I pulled her into a hug. "Let me look into it."

"Thank you Alice." She hugged me back, relieved.

"Go back to the house. And please be careful. If the Sanguis figure out you know their plans, you could be in danger."

Josie nodded, giving me another hug before leaving. I had her go first, then left the baby changing room a minute later. Coming out of the hallway, I bumped into Bret. He scanned me for visible signs of an attack, and when he found none, he sighed and narrowed his gaze.

"You were back there for a long time."

I shrugged off his accusing tone. "Can you find someplace called Jack's? Some Sanguis are meeting there at seven tonight."

"Why would I do that?"

"Because these particular Sanguis were overheard threatening my life."

Conflict flashed in his eyes. Bret sighed, pinching the bridge of his nose, pushing his glasses up his face. "I'll see what I can do."

"I'm sorry I'm adding more work onto your plate."

"I'll have someone else look into that matter." He dropped his hand. "Right now, my instructions are to keep you safe."

I winced at the word. "If you don't want to be here, you can have someone take your place."

"I never said that Miss Thorpe. My Alpha trusts me with you —an honour in itself — but just like him, I don't want you to be attacked again without proper backup."

"So, you both think I'm a weak human?"

"Not at all. Asking for help is not a weakness, and neither is wanting to be saved or protected. On the contrary, Ryan wants to be here for you. He wants you to know he always has your back."

I blinked blurry eyes at him. His words brought a wave of emotions. I was relieved to hear that Bret also doesn't think me weak. Ryan admitted as much this morning. Knowing I have both of them at my back does relieve some of my stress over this vampire situation. Bret offered me a tissue with a small smile. I took it with a laugh. I can't remember the last time I shed tears. Yet here I am, ready to break down after a few simple words.

I composed myself before returning to Patty. "Sorry, that took a while."

"Did you get lost?" Her tone was teasing, but her eyes skittered past me to the hallway.

"There was a line. Then I bumped into Bret coming out. He was worried something happened."

"I've never understood how there is always a line for the women's washroom but never for the men's."

"It's a mystery we women will never figure out."

Patty laughed. "If you're done with your now cold Thai, we can continue shopping."

I took a bite of my food to judge how cold it was. "Yep, I'm done."

"Good." We placed our trays at the cleaning station for an attendant to deal with, then left the food court. "You've done a lot of window shopping. I think it's time you bought something."

"I don't need anything though."

"Not even a piece of lingerie that will bring Ryan to his knees?"

I blushed; an image of his jaw-dropping, as he falls to his knees, danced in my mind. "I'm not getting something for him."

"Then get it for yourself." Patty shifted her shopping bags to one hand to take my arm. "Bringing a man to his knees is a powerful thing."

I shook my head, letting myself get dragged to a lingerie store. Patty was having the time of her life using me like a dress-up doll. I had made a few purchases by the time we left the mall.

My mother had left a dress on my bed. Grimacing, I returned it to my closet and chose something else. I popped ibuprofen and freshened

up. I made a quick stop at the weapons room before making my way downstairs. Standing at the bottom of the stairs, my mother frowned up at me.

"That's not the dress I pulled out for you."

"This one is fine Mother."

"Fine?" She squawked. "It's too casual."

"I think she looks beautiful." My father came up beside her, wrapping an arm around her waist.

"Bret, where will you be?" I turned my attention to the Beta, who was finishing a phone call.

"I'll be outside watching the doors to the restaurant." He responded.

I could have sworn he scowled when the doorbell rang. The expression was so quick that I could have been imagining it. Lucas walked in, gaped at me, and then offered his arm. He escorted me out of the house with a pleasant 'you look beautiful.' He took me to a Greek restaurant, one that my mother loved and was brought to on every possible occasion. The dress she initially chose would have been overkill.

During dinner, I kept my hands to myself, keeping as much distance between myself and Lucas as possible, and kept my answers to his questions short. I found the entire evening uncomfortable. Lucas didn't seem perturbed by my lack of interest. I hurriedly consumed my food, wanting to escape him quickly. After paying for our meal, he caught me by the elbow and guided me toward a park down the block and across the road.

As large of a city as Stellacote is, the mayor has always insisted on having parks scattered around the city. These well-maintained parks allow people to escape the city without leaving the city. This particular park contains a pond where people can be found feeding the ducks that like to swim in it during the day. While at night, it is lit for a romantic stroll.

"Let me go Lucas." I hissed, pulling free of his grip. "I want to go home. I don't want to marry you. Nothing you do will change my mind."

"What is so wrong with me that you won't give me a chance?"

"For starters, you forced a kiss on me the first time we met. Then twenty-four hours later, you're on your knee proposing marriage. I don't love you. I don't even like you."

"One doesn't have to be in love to marry; in time, you'll come to like me." He countered.

"I don't even want to be in the same room as you."

"I'm not going to give up on you. You'll come to see that marrying me has its benefits."

"What benefits?" I scowled.

A growl came from behind us. I spun to see wolf eyes staring at me from the alley beside the restaurant. I shoved at Lucas.

"Run!"

I know running is stupid, but I can't fight a wolf with Lucas right there. I didn't expect him to take my hand and pull me across the street into the park. The wolf followed. It didn't even bother running. At least not until it hit the park's edge, then it sprang for me. I was able to twist myself free from Lucas just as the wolf pounced on me, knocking me to the ground.

Stars bloomed behind my eyes at the pain that shot through my back. I vaguely heard Lucas say something about the police or animal control. I wasn't sure. I was too busy holding the wolf's jaw away from my neck with both hands. The wolf's eyes seemed to glow blue, just like Carden's, I'd never seen a wolf with blue eyes before, and it sent an icy chill down my spine. I needed a free hand to get a dagger from under my dress to defend myself. With quite a bit of effort, I got my feet under it and pushed the wolf far enough away that I got access to a dagger. I got one blade into its neck when he was suddenly off me.

Scrambling up, I stared at the sight of two wolves fighting. I wasn't going to get in the middle of that fight. Taking Lucas's hand, I ran out of the park and back to his car. He seemed too stunned by what was happening behind us to unlock the vehicle. I snapped at him. He stared at me blankly. Irritated, I took his keys, pushed him into the back and drove home. It wasn't until I reached for my clutch that I realized it was probably in the park.

# CHAPTER NINE

## RYAN

THE FIRST THING I did when I got off the plane was turn on my phone. There was a missed call from Bret. I listened to the voice message he'd left me. An update to tell me that there has been no movement from Alice's attacker and that she's asked him to look into a possible threat from some Sanguis. That is a surprise. Queen should have better control over her enforcer vampires. I don't have time to worry about them right now. I'll trust Bret to handle the situation. I'm more concerned that the killer vampire hasn't made a move yet. There's no way he's left Stellacote, or Alice, alone.

I deleted the voicemail. Being away from Alice gutted me. I need to find Roman, talk to him about this vampire and why I wasn't warned of any potential attacks, then return to her. The longer I'm away from my Hunter, the more I worry about what might happen without me by her side. Bret will protect her. I do not doubt my Beta's strength and loyalty. I was about to dial Roman's number when my phone rang. Speak of the devil.

"About time you call me." I growled.

"About time you got here. Now hurry up. I don't have all day."

Roman ended the call abruptly. I stared at my phone, processing what he said. I don't know how, but somehow he knew I was here in France. Thankfully Bret packed me a carry-on bag, so there was no need to head to the baggage corral. Stepping outside the airport, I looked around. Roman was leaning against a black SUV in the pick-up line, waiting for me. Despite being an Alpha myself, Roman still sets off inner warnings of danger.

"How did you know I was here?" I demanded as I approached.

Roman's lips twitched. "I knew it would only be a matter of time before you came."

I frowned. "Are you working with the vampire?"

Roman growled menacingly, pushing off the SUV. "Get in."

I hesitated. I need answers. Making a very public scene will not get me any answers I seek. With my guard up, I slid into the passenger seat as Roman went around to the driver's side. He drove in silence to the countryside, where the properties were massive and private. The house Roman pulled up to was a simple brick two-story building with ivy growing up the walls. Warning bells went off even louder than earlier in my mind. This place is secluded. If I don't return home in a couple of days, Bret will never know where to start looking for my corpse — if Roman is really working with the vampire, which I don't honestly believe is true. One can never be too careful.

Roman parked the SUV. A strawberry-blonde woman stepped out of the house with a shotgun. She aimed it at the vehicle. I stared at her through the windshield. Roman opened his door, stepping out of the SUV, and I got a whiff of a human. I caught a brief exhale when she saw Roman. She shifted her feet, the gun barrel aimed in my direction. I stayed where I sat.

"Put the gun down Jacqueline." Roman ordered.

"Who did you bring with you Roman?" The woman — Jacqueline — demanded.

"A fellow Alpha." Roman told her. "Can you make us something to eat? It's been a long flight for him."

She hesitated. When she didn't lower the shotgun, Roman walked over to her, placed his hand on the barrel and lowered it himself. She looked up at him. There was something between them. Not a word was said. They stared at each other a long moment before she turned and marched back into the house. Roman turned to look at me, silently telling me to hurry up and get out of the SUV. Bag in hand, I complied.

"Where exactly are we?" I questioned Roman as I approached. "And who is that woman?"

"Jacqueline." Roman said without giving me any more information.

I scowled at the Alpha. If this is how things are going to go, getting answers will be like pulling teeth. He went inside, leaving the front door open for me to follow. I hesitated, glancing back at the SUV, debating between returning to the airport and returning to Alice. I clenched my jaw. Alice is why I'm here in the first place. I need answers, answers that I'm pretty sure Roman has. I followed into the house. The inside looked cottage cozy. I heard voices from further in the house, and I followed them to a kitchen.

Roman stood with his arms crossed over his chest and leaning back against some cupboards. Jacqueline was busy stirring something in a large pot. Two boys, possibly around twelve, were sitting at an island. They looked up at me when I entered the space. Jacqueline shooed them out of the kitchen, so it was just the three of us. The tension was palpable.

"Those are her sons, Lyle and Gaige." Roman belatedly introduced.

"Roman." Jacqueline scolded.

"He can be trusted."

I extended my hand. "Ryan Lune."

She eyed my hand suspiciously before tentatively accepting the gesture. "Jacqueline Couvier."

"A pleasure." I looked between her and Roman. "I don't mean to sound rude, but are you and Roman?"

"Heavens, no!" She exclaimed, insulted.

"Her husband, Roy, is a detective and a Hunter leader." Roman explained.

"Where are you from?"

"Stellacote."

Jacqueline's eyes widened, and her shoulders stiffened. "Then you know Jeffery Thorpe."

"I do." I nodded.

"Are he and his family okay?"

"Yes." Not sure if she knows about the vampire, so I didn't elaborate.

"Good." She sighed, relieved, then returned her focus to the stove.

"There's something I have to show you." Roman stated.

He walked me to a large dining room table and ordered me to sit. I placed my bag on the floor next to me and sat. Roman left the room and returned with stacks of files in his hands. He put them in front of me and then took a seat opposite.

"When Roy heard about his fellow Hunter in Japan going missing, he had me take in his family as he looked into it." Roman began. "These files contain both his research and mine. Roy dropped it off the day before his disappearance. I reviewed them, warned Charlie, and then continued to add to it as best I could."

"Yet you didn't warm me." I stated bitterly.

Roman shrugged. With a glare to satisfy my annoyance at his negligence in warning me, I then turned my attention to the files. I opened the first file. It contained information on the first killings in Japan, police reports, autopsies, and newspaper articles. Thankfully all translated into English. The following file contained information on the next family to be murdered in Japan. Two more files for murders in Japan, all different cities, as the vampire tried to find the Hunter leader. Four innocent families were murdered before reaching the Hunter leader.

I read every piece of paper in the files, including what I assumed were Roy's handwritten notes and questions he wanted answers to. Jacqueline placed a bowl of soup down and sat beside Roman. The smell was delicious. I pulled the soup in closer to eat while I continued to read. Neither one of them spoke as I reviewed all the information. Most of the information within the Japan files is what I already know from what I've gathered about the murders in Stellacote.

The next set of files was for murders in Europe. Roy must have figured it was Hunter leaders being targeted and had Roman take in his family so they weren't part of the murder spree. Again, four innocent families were lost to this crime spree. The last file held a single piece of paper with a handwritten note saying Australia would be the next target.

"Is this why you warned Charlie and not me?" I questioned Roman.

The man scowled. "I had no idea who would be the target after Charlie."

"How much information do you know that's not in these files?"

Roman glanced at Jacqueline. "All I know is that a vampire is leading some sort of hunt on Hunter leaders."

"Do you have a map? I'd like to see exactly where each of these murders took place."

Roman raised a questioning brow but didn't verbally question me. I want to see if there's a pattern, like the one that seemed to be happening in Capital Hill. Roman left the table and returned with three maps: one for Japan, one for Europe, and a third for Australia. Markings showed where each murder had taken place.

Japan's murders were sporadic. Those in Europe were a little neater, showing one in Italy, another in Austria, a third in Germany and then two in France — a star shape, just like what Bret and I saw. The Australian murders were in the same pattern but condensed into one area.

The vampire's attack on the Hunter leaders continuously became more straightforward and precise. By the time he reached Stellacote, he had perfected how he wanted the murders of the innocent to be portrayed. Disturbing.

"How did Roy predict that Australia would be attacked after Europe?" I looked up from the Australian map.

"Jacqueline?"

The woman in question played with a locket around her neck. "There's a hierarchy within the Hunter leaders. Africa is at the bottom, followed by Asia, Europe, Australia, South America, and then North America is at the top. Each continent has one Hunter leader that rules over all the other Hunters in that continent. Think of them as the Alpha, then within various cities or quadrants — however their continent is divided — is then run by a Captain, like a Beta."

"Then why would these killings not affect Africa and South America?" I pondered, pushing the now empty bowl aside. "Something doesn't add up."

"It is strange the killing spree doesn't go in order of weakest to strongest." Roman agreed. "What do you know that's not in this file?"

I took a moment to organize my thoughts before diving into some facts. "I noticed a pattern to the killing spree within my city; it's to lure the Hunter out. Each murder scene matched the Hunter family. From the files you showed me, the killer went after four innocent families before reaching the Hunter. The vampire on this killing spree slipped up. It attacked my Hunter too soon."

Jacqueline gasped. "You said Jeffery is okay."

"He is. I got a description of the vampire: golden blond hair and blue eyes. According to Charlie, when his Hunter disappeared, he picked up the scent of wolves, vampires, and other humans."

"That coordinates with what happened here." Roman added. "If Roy wasn't anticipating an attack, I'm sure it would have been a massacre. Thankfully the only one in the house was him. He had let all the staff go when he charged me with protecting Jacqueline and his sons. I've had my wolves on the hunt for Roy since."

"Is that why you never called me back?"

"I was busy keeping the peace. Relations between wolves and vampires are rocky, and I didn't want a war to erupt in the middle of the streets." Roman scowled. "As much as I'd like to tear those blood suckers limb from limb, I owe Roy. So I'm fighting my instincts."

I blinked in surprise. Roman is a far cry from a peacekeeper. There's a story there that I'd love to dive into, but now isn't the time. I need as much information as possible before I go back to Alice. Knowing about past murders is helpful, but it's not what I need right now to protect Alice. What I need is more information on the Hunter Society. Jeffery won't give me information, but a wife worried about her husband might.

"Jeffery only recently learned about his fellow Hunters going missing." I explained. "He said communication is limited with other Hunters as they've gone into survival mode. He also believes they've been betrayed."

"By who?" Jacqueline questioned, surprised.

"No clue, but only a Hunter would know who the Hunter leaders are. Someone has told this vampire where to find them and how many are in their family. Someone wants the leaders gone."

"Mother."

We all looked to the entry into the kitchen. Both of Jaqueline's sons stood there with determined looks on their faces. Brave boys. They are far too young to be involved in monster matters.

"Gaige, sweetie, you shouldn't be down here." Jacqueline went over to her sons. "You and Lyle should be upstairs."

Gaige frowned, hands clenched at his sides. "I want to help save Father."

"Me too." Lyle stated a little too loudly.

"Oh, boys." Jacqueline pulled them in for a hug. "As proud as your father would be to hear that, he wants you to be safe. That's why he has Roman protecting us."

"But we're tired of sitting here." Gaige complained.

"We want to help." Lyle added.

"You're no match for this vampire." I told them sternly. "My Hunter barely survived fighting him."

"We're strong." Gaige insisted.

"I'm sure you are. My Hunter is more than twice your age, with more training and was still thrown around like a rag doll." I winced at the memory of Alice limp in my arms. "On top of it all, my Hunter was bitten."

Lyle's eyes widened. "The bite got cleaned, right?"

"I barely made it in time, but yes. My Hunter is still in one piece, and the vampire hasn't evaded my Hunter's mind." Although I couldn't be sure of that statement, Alice said the vampire was calling her last night. "You wouldn't want your father to worry over you?"

"No." They chimed solemnly.

Then Gaige replied. "We still want to help."

"How about tomorrow you two help me keep the peace with the vampires here in France?" Roman suggested. "It's what your father wants."

They nodded eagerly, then turned, leaving the room with proclamations to train. I watched them go with a frown. Was Alice that eager to follow in her father's footsteps when she was that young? It just doesn't seem right to have children train to fight monsters when the monsters are fighting to keep the peace — or fighting among themselves.

Jacqueline returned to her seat. "Thank you, I can't lose them too."

"Roy will return." Roman promised, resting a hand over hers.

She smiled faintly and then turned to me. "Your Hunter, I noticed you never stated it was Jeffery."

"That's because it's not." I hesitated. "The Hunter of Stellacote is Alice."

Her eyes widened. "His daughter? I remember Roy saying that Jeffery was making a bold move. That was twenty-two years ago. I had no idea what he was talking about."

"Maybe that bold move is the source of today's issues."

Her expression changed to thoughtful. "Roy also mentioned that they had publicly announced that they were kicking out a member. That member didn't take it well."

"Do you know that member's name?"

Jacqueline closed her eyes, concentrating, then slowly said the name. "Alex Kingsley."

Kingsley. I know that name. Closing my eyes, I thought it over. Kingsley is one of the families in Capital Hill. I had Baxter make a list of all the families in the gated community to attempt to determine who was next in the killings after the second attack. Then it hit me — Lucas. His name was on that list. My stomach clenched. I have to get back to Stellacote. Immediately. I picked up my bag and stood.

"Where are you going?"

"I need to get back to Stellacote." I told them. "Alice is in more danger than just the vampire."

# CHAPTER TEN

## ALICE

I WOKE FROM A relatively peaceful sleep. I rolled onto my back. The sudden pressure on the injury jolted me awake. I rolled to my side quickly, tears stinging my eyes. My back will never heal with all the abuse it keeps going under. No longer able to stay in bed, I sat up. I stretched my arms over my head, feeling every ache my body had to offer. Turning, I lifted the sheets to slip out of bed and froze. In the middle of my bedroom floor lay a wolf.

My breath caught in my throat after a sharp intake. The wolf watched me, his head resting on its front paws. I forced myself to breathe. At least it didn't have the same eerie blue eyes as the wolf that attacked me last night. Maintaining eye contact and moving slowly, I reached for the bedside table. Patting the surface for a dagger, I thought I'd left there when my hand knocked something off. I looked at the floor to see my clutch.

"Did you bring this back?" I looked back up at the wolf.

It just blinked at me. I didn't sense this wolf to be a threat, so I kicked the sheets off, swung my legs over the edge and bent to pick up the clutch. If the wolf was going to attack me, it would have by now. A sudden knock on my bedroom door had the wolf standing. Lucas strolled in without an invitation, his eyes widening at the sight of the wolf, and he raised a gun. The wolf growled, its ears flattening as it positioned itself between Lucas and me.

"Get away from her!" Lucas clasped the gun with both hands.

It took a moment for me to register the situation. The wolf is protecting me. I pulled a blanket off my bed, wrapped it around me and stood.

"Lucas put the gun away." I told him, exasperated.

"There's a wolf in your room."

"How observant." I replied dryly, coming to stand beside the wolf and tentatively putting a hand on its head. "It's not going to hurt me."

Standing next to the wolf was intimidating. Its back was at the same height as my chest. It was the largest wolf I'd seen so far. I wondered who it could be. I've never seen Ryan in wolf form before, but he's off in France, so it can't be him. It may be Bret. Again, I have never seen him in wolf form. The wolves I've faced before have all been smaller, like teenagers versus adults.

"You were attacked by a wolf last night."

"And we were saved by one." I reminded him.

My father entered behind Lucas, gave a quick look around then scowled. "Put that thing away, boy."

"Does no one care that there is a dangerous wolf in the room?"

"The only dangerous thing about this whole situation is you."

"Me?" Lucas squeaked, turning his body toward My father while keeping a single hand on the gun pointed at the wolf. "How am I dangerous?"

"You have no idea how to use that." He stated flatly, snatching the gun from Lucas's hand with ease, opened the barrel chamber and emptied it of its six bullets. "You could have killed my daughter."

"I don't see that bodyguard with the glasses around to protect her."

I glanced down at the wolf. Its dirty blonde colouring reminded me of Bret's hair. The wolf, no longer growling, gently leaned into me. It has to be Bret. My hand ran through the fur on its head, amazed at Bret's wolf form. I wondered if Ryan's wolf is just as big or even bigger because he's Alpha. Bret's calming aura is just as powerful in wolf form as it is in human form.

"Detective Michaelson is making a tour of the property." My father lied. "He'll be back momentarily."

"Lucas." I drew his attention.

"Yes?" He asked hopefully.

"Get out of my room."

He flushed with embarrassment and was shoved out by my father. When the door closed behind both men, I wrapped my arms around the wolf's neck and whispered a thank you. Then, needing to get ready for the day, I collected some clothes and escaped to the bathroom. When I returned, there was a pile of clothes on my dresser that I assumed my father had brought in for Bret. I took them into the bathroom for him. After the shower ran a second time, Bret returned to my bedroom looking fresh and human.

"Morning Bret." I teased him lightly. "Good to see you."

"Good morning Miss Thorpe." He smiled faintly. "What do you have planned for today?"

"Nothing."

"Would you be so inclined as to accompany me to the station?"

"Am I in trouble?"

"I sent someone to listen in on the Sanguis last night, and I want to know what he learnt. But, after last night's attack and this morning's little encounter, I'm uneasy about leaving you alone."

I nodded in agreement. "Who was that wolf that attacked last night?"

Bret scowled. "Not one of ours."

"Why did it attack me? Why did that wolf have the same blue eyes as that vampire?" I bombarded Bret with questions, and based on how his jaw was set, he knew the answers and refused to tell them. "What are you not telling me?"

"Miss Thorpe, please don't ask me questions I cannot answer."

"Can't or won't?" My irritation of not being informed rose. "Why am I being kept in the dark?"

Bret moved to the bedroom door, opening it for me. "I'm sorry."

I hesitated for a minute before stomping out into the hall. I have to find out what is being kept from me and hope the answer lies with the Sanguis. I marched straight to the front door.

"Oh. Your car." I turned to Bret. "Should we take mine?"

"I had a pack member pick it up from the restaurant." He reached around to open the front door. "See? It's over there in your visitor parking area."

"When did you have that done? Weren't you in wolf form all night?"

"There were a couple of pack members with me last night. One of them was in charge of getting the car here for the morning if I had to shift."

I buckled into the passenger seat. Bret slid in behind the wheel, reaching over to the glove box to pull out a pair of glasses before putting the car into reverse. He kept silent throughout the drive to the station. His silence forced me to stay quiet. Bret won't give me any answers to the many questions I have without Ryan's approval. Ryan and my father have all the answers, yet neither is willing to give them to me.

Bret led me through the station to his shared office. Someone was already inside. I didn't think it was Ryan since he only left for France yesterday. There's no way he was back so soon. If he were back, he would have come to me first — at least, I hope he would. The man inside is young, the same man who took me home a few days ago when I woke up in the station after being attacked by Carden.

"Baxter." Bret greeted.

"Oh!" The young officer turned around, startled. "Detective Michaelson, I wasn't expecting you back to the station so soon."

"Miss Alice Thorpe, this is Baxter Jones." Bret introduced us. "He's a junior detective working his way up in the ranks. I had him go to Jack's last night. It turns out it's a bar — *Jack's Men*."

"What did you learn?" I asked him eagerly.

Baxter frowned, turning toward Bret, who gestured for him to explain. "Seriously? You want a civilian to listen in on police matters?"

I scowled at him, ready with a retort, but Bret intervened. "This civilian informed me of the meeting at Jack's that could put innocent lives in danger."

"How would she know about this?"

"She's an informant."

"She's a Thorpe." He glanced at me. "Who could she be informing on?"

"She." I growled. "Is right here. Whom I inform on is none of your concern, junior detective. Now, what did you learn at Jack's?"

Baxter looked both irritated and flustered. "I don't know."

"What do you mean you don't know?"

"What do you know?" Bret questioned with a hint of irritation in his voice. "What did you hear? What did you see?"

"There was a group of four scary-looking men huddled in a booth. They looked like the kind who would make threats to people's lives. I got as close as I dared, but I didn't understand what they were saying." Baxter explained.

"Well?"

"Here." Baxter fished for his phone from his pocket. "I tried to get a recording of them."

Hitting play, the only thing that could be heard was the bustle of a crowd. Bret took the phone plugging it into his computer. I don't know what he was doing, but when the recording started again, the sound of the crowd was almost non-existent. Baxter snapped his fingers, pointing to the computer, when the low rumble of a male voice spoke.

"How many more Sanguis are willing to stand against Queen?"

"Only a third of them are willing." Someone answered him. "I'm sure more will join us once we make our move."

"Good." The first voice answered. "The Hunters are going down tomorrow night. The vamp said to bring them in alive for experiments but otherwise doesn't care what condition they are brought to him.

He'll be sending some wolves and humans to help. They won't be able to stop all of us."

"What about the Alpha and Beta?" A third voice asked.

"What about them?"

"The Alpha was quite protective of the young Hunter when they came to see Queen."

"The Alpha isn't even in Stellacote, and he won't return until after the attack. As for the Beta, he won't do anything unless he's told to. He's a well-trained wolf."

"Hey!" The second voice called before the recording ended.

"That's all I got." Baxter admitted. "They seemed to be talking in code. I didn't understand a word of it."

Feeling dizzy and sick, I slumped into a chair. I have to get my parents out of the house before the attack tonight. And I have to warn Queen about the uprising within her Sanguis. The men were right, Ryan wouldn't be back in time to stop anything, but I felt I had to warn him. It didn't sound like Carden was going to be at the attack. If I can find him before the attack, maybe I can stop it or convince him to leave my parents alone.

"Whatever you're thinking Miss Thorpe." Bret broke through my thoughts. "Stop."

I looked up at him. He was glaring at me. "But the attack."

"We would stop it if we knew whom they were talking about." Baxter stated.

I jumped when Baxter spoke, forgetting he was in the room. He obviously isn't privy to the supernatural world. Very few humans are.

"Baxter, get Miss Thorpe a soothing cup of peppermint tea." Bret ordered, waiting for the junior detective to leave before speaking again.

"I'll have your parents moved before nightfall, and I'll contact Ryan. He contacted me yesterday. He'll be returning to Stellacote soon. His trip to France was useful."

"What about Queen?"

"There is no way she doesn't know what's going on in her own house."

I nodded, but I couldn't shake the feeling of dread. Everything Bret said was reassuring, but it didn't help. I still felt a need to go after Carden and do something myself. Baxter returned with the tea. I breathed in the scent but didn't drink it as Bret did some paperwork.

When Bret finished and was ready to take me home, Captain Forest demanded to see him. I stayed in the office with Baxter keeping an eye on me. I didn't pay him any attention. My mind was still off in the distance, trying to figure out how I could lure Carden into a trap. He's been able to stay hidden from Queen, from Ryan, and from me. There is no way he'd step out of hiding for no good reason. The only thing I kept coming back to is that I'd never get a second chance at facing off with Carden when I have a bodyguard.

It was late afternoon by the time Bret and I finally made it back to my house. I made my way upstairs as Bret went in search of my father. I stared at my bedroom from the hall. I couldn't bring myself to pack a bag and go to a safe house with my parents. Shifting direction, I went to my father's study and down to the weapons room. I prepared for battle; daggers in my boots, on my legs and arms, a sword attached to my hip, and a mini crossbow on my wrist. I stared at the framed map of the city. Behind it is a safe containing dangerous weapons that can kill a vampire or werewolf nearly instantly. The downside to these weapons: I'd have to get close to the target.

I slipped out through a hidden door in the training room. The dirt-packed tunnel led to the shed at the farthest reaches of the yard. Climbing up into the shed, I looked out its small window to see that no one had noticed me missing. Then, knowing it won't be long before Bret starts to track me, I rushed out of the shed and into the trees surrounding our property. I ran straight for the dirt road between my house and the neighbours. Parked on the side of the road covered by a tarp and fallen tree branches is a car I left there for when I went into the city without my mother's knowledge. I keep the keys in the glove box, locked by an electronic key on my phone.

I floored it down the dirt road coming out a street away from my house. I have no idea where I am going, but I felt something directing me away from my house and away from the city to the farmland. I slowed down only when I hit traffic. Cursing, I looked around at my surroundings. Whatever feeling had guided me had led me to the Richardson Farm.

Two generations ago, the Richardson family struggled to keep their farm running. Then, one night they set up a sheet as a screen and invited friends over to watch a movie. It's said that's when the idea to open their farm as a drive-in theatre came to them. As the years went by and business blossomed, they were able to add amenities which helped them bring in more revenue.

I followed the crowd of cars into the farm, paying the five-dollar flat fee to enter. I found a spot off to the side and got out. I scanned the area, trying to figure out why I was pulled to this farm.

A voice in my head sent a shiver down my spine as it called me. It was Carden. I closed my eyes, shaking my head. I don't want his voice in my head. He kept calling me, his voice sounding close. Part of me wanted to find him, while another part wanted to run away. I steeled myself, slowly opening my eyes, afraid he would be standing there. Nothing. The farmland filled up quickly while I had my eyes closed.

The trailers began as the sun set behind the large screen the Richardson family purchased during the peak of drive-in theatres. They had to wait for movies to make it to DVD, so everything they played was at least two years old. That never stopped the crowd from coming.

"Miss Thorpe!" A dangerous growl escaped whoever took my arm in a painful grip.

I instinctively pulled out a dagger turning to face the unknown male, aiming for the heart when Bret grabbed my wrist. He glared, a look I was not used to seeing on him. Bret is not happy with me.

"What do you think you're doing?"

"Bret. You startled me."

He let go of my wrist so I could put the dagger away.

"What are you doing? I had Baxter track your phone when I realized you weren't in your room. Or in the house. I was afraid the vampire had gotten to you in the short time I wasn't at your side." His tone was a mix of anger and fear.

I scowled, looking away. "I wasn't going to go into hiding with my parents. I can't do that."

"I never said you should." He rubbed the bridge of his nose with a sigh. "Ryan may have fought with you about that, but eventually, he would have caved. You can be just as stubborn as my Alpha. I, on the other hand, would have asked you what you needed."

"Oh." I sheepishly looked back at him, embarrassed for running away from him now. "The vampire is close. He's here somewhere."

"How do you know?"

"I just do."

Bret's eyes focused on the cornfield past my car. "I would suggest looking there first. With all eyes on the screen, he could slip in and out for a bite before anyone noticed."

I nodded. Dread filled me as I closely followed Bret into the cornfield, a dagger at the ready. The faint sound of the movie playing could still be heard the further we travelled into the cornfield. Bret's arm suddenly shot out, stopping me from going any further. His body crouched, primed to attack. A soft curse from Bret, and he scooped me up, running away from the direction we were heading but not in the direction of the open field. I looked over his shoulder as he carried me bridal style. Two wolves came chasing after us, both with blue eyes.

I struggled to get my phone free from my back pocket. Sending an SOS text to Ryan so that when he lands, he'll know he'll need to start searching for me immediately. Another curse from Bret as he stumbled and forced himself to continue. Shifting my position in Bret's arms, I threw the dagger I held toward the wolf. It whimpered as the blade implanted itself in its shoulder joint. I got another dagger ready to throw at the other wolf but couldn't see it over Bret's shoulder.

He stopped suddenly. I turned to see a blue-eyed wolf, and Carden was standing before us, blocking our path. The injured wolf came up behind us, stopping our retreat. Bret put me down beside him, a protective arm out, but there was no way to be safe in this situation. I focused my attention on Carden. He is the most dangerous one among the three.

"I'm so pleased you came to see me Alice." Carden grinned. "Though the werewolf was uncalled for."

There was a popping sound, and Bret hunched forward.

"Bret!" I grabbed his arm.

"Stubborn."

Two more popping sounds, and Bret fell.

"Much better."

"No! Bret!" I followed him down, shaking his immobile body.

"He's not dead, just knocked out. Three tranquillizers to put him down, that's quite impressive." Carden mused.

I bolted to my feet. I have to put the wolves down first before I can even think of going after Carden. I don't understand why they are even working with him. None of this makes sense. My hand twitched over the handle of my sword, wondering if I could draw it before any of them attacked me.

"Don't do anything stupid Alice." Carden drawled, pointing a tranquillizer gun at me. "You know what, I'm not going to risk it."

He fired the tranquillizer while he spoke. I barely had my sword drawn an inch when it hit me in the chest. I stared at it, somewhat confused, as the tranquillizer took effect. Then, my vision blurred, and Carden's smile was the last thing I saw before everything went black.

# Chapter Eleven

## Ryan

I ITCHED TO GET off the plane and get back to Alice. Instinct warned me that something went wrong while I was away. The second I was allowed to turn on my phone, I checked for voice messages. Bret left me a couple of messages. One informed me of Alice's attack the night before and the wolf he and the pack were able to capture because of it. Another updated me about some of the Sanguis teaming up with the vampire to attack the Thorpes, so he'll be moving them to a safe house. Finally, Alice sent me an SOS text.

Heart in my throat, I tried calling her, but it went to voice mail after four rings. Next, I tried Bret. His phone went straight to voice mail. I rushed out of the airport to my car, nearly knocking people down in my haste, and drove straight to the Thorpe house. When I arrived, fire trucks were finishing putting out flames. The house was barely holding itself up. Captain Forest frowned at the scene. I marched over to him.

"What happened?" I demanded.

I couldn't bring myself to ask the other terrifying questions floating in my head. Not yet anyway.

"Thank goodness you're back." Hugh sighed, turning to me. "I don't know. Around three this morning, neighbours called 9-1-1. The fire was going strong, and the firemen struggled to get it under control. Now that the fire is almost out, we're going to do a sweep around the house for evidence. Have you talked to your partner yet?"

"I haven't been able to get a hold of him." I admitted, unable to tear my eyes off the scene. "Any hint that people were inside?"

He shook his head. "Michaelson told me yesterday he was putting the Thorpe's up in a safe house. I hope he was able to get to them in time."

"Captain Forest." The fire chief came over. "We found bodies."

"How many?"

"So far, a dozen."

The two continued to talk as they walked toward the house. I couldn't bring myself to follow them. There's no way Alice or her parents are the remains in that fire. That vampire, and Alex Kingsley, wouldn't let that happen. This fire is a distraction to cover evidence and to get away. I have to find Alice before it's too late. Returning to my car, I called Baxter, mentally praying he was at the station.

"Baxter, it's Ryan." I breathed a sigh of relief when he picked up.

"Detective Lune." He exclaimed surprised. "When did you get back?"

"Just now. Are you at the station?"

"I am. What do you need me to do?"

"Trace Alice Thorpe's phone." I ordered.

"Again?" Baxter groaned. "What is it about this woman?"

"What do you mean again?" My heart dropped to my stomach.

"Detective Michaelson had me trace her phone yesterday."

She went missing yesterday? When did she leave Bret's sight? Did he find her? So many questions and so few answers, and time was ticking. I'm already behind. Baxter's voice returned on the line pulling me from the spiral my mind was taking.

"There we go. She's at the Kingsley's house."

That can't be good. "Send me the address."

"Detective Lune, what's going on?"

"Just send me the address Baxter."

I bit the order out far more harshly than I should have. The junior detective sucked in a sharp breath before rattling off the address. I hung up, put the car into drive, and weaved out of the Thorpe driveway. The Kingsley's lived a few streets over. I recognized the vehicle Alice always drove whenever I went to her apartment, sitting in their driveway. Looking through the windshield, I was relieved that there was no blood, and her phone sat in the cupholder.

Alice wouldn't leave her phone behind. Something isn't right. Taking the front steps two at a time, I rang the doorbell impatiently. When there was no answer in the first thirty seconds, I rang again and again until a butler finally answered. At least, I assumed it was a butler. All these Capital Hill families seem to have a servant for every task in the house.

"Yes?" The old man drawled in a monotone voice, his face showing the slightest bit of irritation.

"Where is Alice Thorpe?" I pushed the door open wider and stepped inside.

"Who, sir? This is the Kingsley residence."

"I know where I am. Where's the woman that drives that car?"

I pointed outside. The man peered out of the door. With a nod, he shut the door, leaving me in the entryway as he went upstairs. I secretly sniffed and was relieved not to find Alice's candy apple scent in the house. Or at least not in the entryway. The butler's voice drifted down to me.

"Master Lucas. A gentleman here wishes to speak with your lady friend."

I could hear some mumbling and shuffling before Lucas came into view. Rubbing his eyes, he stopped at the top of the stairs. Once focused on me, Lucas grinned. The butler didn't come back into view. I could only assume he made himself scarce now that his master was tending to the unwanted guest.

"Detective Lune, what are you doing here?"

"Where is Alice?"

"Keep your voice down." He strolled down the stairs as cocky as ever in a pair of pyjama pants. "You'll wake her."

My hands flexed at my side. "I'm only trying to find her to tell her some unfortunate news."

"What might that be? I'll be sure to pass it along when she wakes."

"Lucas?" A groggy female voice sounded from the top of the stairs. "What is going on? I thought you said we'd be alone."

"Alice." He smiled up at the woman in a dress shirt that barely covered her. "I'm sorry we woke you."

"What are you doing here?" She asked, her gaze flickering between Lucas and me.

With a whiff, I knew this wasn't Alice. This woman smelt of vanilla and not candy apples, though she is a decent look-a-like. It made me sick. I couldn't hold back my disgust with this man. No, not a man, he's just a worthless male, and I'm glad Alice didn't fall for his attempts to charm her. I punched Lucas, satisfaction rushing through me with the action. I've wanted to do that since I first saw him with Alice in his arms. The woman shrieked, running down the stairs to Lucas's side. I turned my back on the sickening scene. I have to find Alice. If I can taunt him enough, Lucas Kingsley might lead me straight to her. Her car being here is no mere coincidence.

"Jealousy doesn't look good on you, detective." Lucas called after me.

I looked over my shoulder, raking my eyes over the woman, and scowled. "Sleeping with a look-a-like won't be the same as the real thing. Trust me."

Lucas flushed. I'd just riled him up. I want him to question Alice about the comment. I'll follow him to find her. As I slipped back into my car, I wished Alice and I had slept together. That intimate connection would have connected us in a way that would help me to track her down on my own. For now, I'll have to find a spot and wait for Lucas to make a move.

I was careful to keep my distance and not get caught by the young Kingsley as I followed him through the city. Finally, he parked at Stellacote University, the science department, to be exact. Horrifying images of Alice and Bret being experimented on flew through my mind. Parking at the back of the parking lot, I texted Hugh that I found a possible lead on my missing partner at Stellacote University, then left my phone in the car. If I go missing next, at least someone will know where to start looking. I took my gun from the glove box and went to the building.

I approached the door from the side, peeking inside to check that the coast was clear before entering. Lucas was nowhere in sight, leaving me to depend on my nose to find him. Just beneath Lucas's grassy scent was the scent of bleach — too much of it to have been from a janitor's cleaning rounds. I tried not to think of the reasons that much bleach would need to be used. Closing my eyes, I refocused on Lucas's scent.

I followed the scent down two hallways, checking around each corner to ensure it was clear before I moved forward. Unfortunately, the building was too quiet. Not even the sound of machines humming softly could be heard through the doors I passed. Turning down a third hallway, I lost Lucas's scent at an elevator. I cursed while pushing the call button. There's no way to tell what floor Lucas could have stopped off at. The doors opened, and I stepped into the metal box. Glancing at the panel, I saw two buttons; one lit which I assumed was for the floor I am currently on, and one below that. I pushed the button, holding my gun up, ready to defend against whatever I was about to face.

The doors opened, and a guard came into view as I stepped off. I shot the guard in the shoulder before he could reach for the gun at his waist. The sound echoed off the walls drawing the attention of more guards. I heard their footsteps coming down the hall.

A fog began filling the space around me, disrupting my vision. Little red lights covered me in various spots: shoulders, legs, and chest. I couldn't see the enemy. If I fired my gun, I could accidentally kill one of them. I heard the popping sound of four guns going off. I stumbled. I didn't feel any stinging from a bullet. Looking at my shoulder, I noticed what appeared to be a dart sticking out of me. My blurred vision darkened as I felt myself falling forward. My gun clattered to the ground.

My last coherent thought was of Alice. This has to be where she is. Then everything went completely black.

# Chapter Twelve

## Alice

My head pounded painfully. I gripped my head with my hands, holding it as if to stop it from rolling off my neck. I sat up. My stomach churned. Keeping my eyes closed, I took careful breaths, refusing to open my eyes until everything settled.

"Alice?" A female voice asked quietly, tentatively.

Slowly I opened my eyes and turned to the voice. "Mother?"

"Thank goodness." She pulled me into a hug. "I was so afraid when they brought you here unconscious."

I frowned, looking around the padded wall room with no windows, a single door, and two chairs with a rug that I was currently sitting on. "Where are we?"

"I'm not sure."

"How long was I out?"

My mother frowned. "I don't know."

I reached for my phone, cursing when it wasn't in my back pocket. Then I looked at myself. My weapons are missing — even the ones in my boots. My mother looked dirty and tired. I got up unsteadily and staggered to the door. Slamming the side of my fist on the door a couple of times, I pressed my ear to it to see if there was any movement on the other side.

"What are you doing?" She questioned me, almost panicked.

"Seeing if I can get someone's attention."

There was the faintest sound of footsteps which halted. A metal slot opened at my feet as a food tray slid in.

"I'm awake." I called out.

There was a brief hesitation before the slot closed. I scowled at the food as my stomach growled. I definitely missed a meal, or maybe two. I put a hand to my stomach. When was the last time I ate? My mother had moved to fetch the food and then returned to a chair, nibbling on a quarter of a sandwich.

"Come, eat something."

I eyed the food, ultimately deciding to take a quarter of the sandwich myself. "Where's Father?"

"They separated us shortly after we arrived."

I frowned. "Who are they?"

"There were four of them." My mother's gaze was fixed somewhere beyond me. "They brought us here. Your father was so brave."

I resigned myself to the fact that I wouldn't get much out of her. Four. I wondered if that would have been the four Sanguis that met at Jack's. All of this was somehow connected to Carden. Just then, I remembered Bret and hoped he was okay and subconsciously rubbed at my chest, where I was hit with the tranquillizer.

The sound of locks being turned had me turning to the door as it swung open. I recognized the two Sanguis as they dragged a bloodied and bruised man into the room. They scowled at me and retreated from the room — for now.

My mother and I dropped to our knees beside him. "Father!"

"Alice." He reached out for my hand, his voice rough. "They want to break us."

"Nothing they do could break me."

"Keep that strength. They have our allies."

"What did they do to you?" My mother teared up, running her fingers gently along his face.

"They want submission. They want to break us."

The locks clicked. I peered over my shoulder to see Carden enter.

He looked at me. "Your turn."

I stood against my mother's protests and followed the blue-eyed blond vampire. He held my arm through white hallways with numbered doors. I kept darting my eyes around for some exit. He stopped at what appeared to be an entertainment room; decorated in warm colours, comfy chairs, and a TV. I couldn't tell who the two people were who sat in the chairs watching the TV. Glancing at the screen, I watched someone shift from human to wolf. I felt sick as the body contorted into a larger shape.

"Bring her over here." One of the people, with a cold male voice ordered.

The vampire tugged my arm, guiding me in front of them, and my eyes widened. "Lucas?"

He narrowed his gaze at me. "Did you sleep with that detective?"

I blinked at the question, could feel my cheeks heat up and shook my head vigorously. "No."

"I told you." The older man beside him grinned. "Hunters stick with their own."

"Who are you?" I turned to the other man, a niggling sensation in the back of my head telling me I'd seen him before.

"Your father-in-law, Alex Kingsley."

I scowled at the bold statement. Then my brows knitted together as the name sunk in. It sounded so familiar. His pale green eyes were the same shade as Lucas' but harsher, as though he's been through some extreme life events.

"Kingsley?"

He nodded. "You and my son will bring about a new generation of Hunters."

I remembered the lists of names my father had me memorize. One contained the name of every Hunter in the society, while the other was for all those kicked out. His name was on that list.

"You're no Hunter." I sneered.

He scowled. "When you marry my son, our name will return to the Hunter Society list."

"I'm not marrying Lucas." I turned to Lucas. "I'm not marrying you."

Fury flooded his face. "Why the hell not? We would be a powerful couple."

"I don't want power."

"Sit down Miss Thorpe." Alex ordered calmly. "Let's discuss the terms rationally."

Carden pushed a comfy chair to my knees. With his hands on my shoulders, he forced me to sit. Something isn't right. Carden can't be working for the Kingsley's? He's far more powerful than they are. They must have some way of controlling him. Or maybe he's using them. My mind raced to figure out who truly worked for whom and what was happening.

"What are you really after?" I glared at Mr. Kingsley. Out of the two, he is the one in charge.

"I want to restructure the Hunter Society. Over the years, they've gone soft and weak. I want to bring us back to our glory days."

"What does that have to do with me?"

He smiled serenely. "We can't successfully do that from the outside."

"What did you do to my father?"

Mr. Kingsley's smile cracked, his hatred seeping through. "I tried to get him to reverse his judgment on me. I tried to have him see things my way, but he wouldn't listen. Called me a barbarian stuck in the past."

He paused, seemingly done talking, so I asked again. "What did you do to my father?"

"Oh." He jolted, seeming startled as if his previous answer was obvious. "I let him spend a couple of hours with one of those savage beasts he refuses to hunt down. I wanted to show him why he needs to side with me."

I recalled how my father looked and scowled. "Why side with a vampire?"

"We have the same interests." He smiled brightly again. "So, Miss Thorpe, will you marry my son and help us rebuild the Hunter Society?"

I seethed. I wanted to show them what I thought of their offer, but I couldn't without a weapon and the vampire still holding me down. There were still some things that didn't make sense to me. Such as:

Why me? There were a few other female Hunters they could use. Were all those innocent deaths part of their plan? And why? I still don't understand why Carden, someone that seems to have Queen scared, was working with them.

"Alice." Lucas came over to me, brushing a hand along my cheek. "I promise to treat you like royalty."

He cupped my chin, lifting my face to his. Lucas braced himself on the chair arm as he leaned in to kiss me. I raised my leg, kicking him in the family jewels. He had kissed me once, and I wouldn't let that happen again. Lucas groaned in pain, stepping away from me and glaring.

"No."

"Send her to our newest beastly monster." Lucas gritted through clenched teeth. "A couple of hours with it might change her mind."

As Carden forced me to stand, I glanced at the TV where the now fully formed werewolf was viciously trying to break down the door. "The only monsters I see are in this room."

Carden growled as he shifted his grip from my shoulders to my arm and led me out of the room. "I'll let the wolf play with you for a little while. Then you're mine."

"I belong to no one."

"I'm already in your head Alice." He stopped to spin me around, then leaned in, running his fangs along my neck. "You can't fight me, and soon you'll come to me willingly."

Fear had me frozen in place. His fangs poked my neck, but they didn't pierce my skin. He ran his tongue on the spot before he kept walking. I stumbled as he tugged me along, unsure why he didn't bite me again. I'm convinced he has his own plans. The Kingsleys are unknowingly helping him do something. What I have to do with it, I have no idea.

"Why me?"

He didn't answer.

"Why is someone as powerful as you working for weak humans like the Kingsley's?"

"We have a similar goal." Carden answered. "Soon, they will no longer be needed."

The white corridors suddenly turned to grey concrete. Carden stopped at a large steel door, punched in a code on the keypad then continued. The scent of blood hit my nose as screams and howls bombarded my ears. The vampire didn't go very far down the hall of steel doors when he finally stopped at one. He punched in another code, and I could hear the sound of a bolt unlatching. Carden pushed me through and closed the door behind me.

I stumbled into another door that vibrated beneath my touch. Suddenly that door opened, and I was faced with a werewolf. I had never seen a wolf as big as him before. It was even larger than Bret. The brown wolf growled at me. I put my hands up, staying perfectly still as the wolf hunched, looking like he was ready to pounce on me.

My eyes darted up to the camera in the far corner. I have to destroy that feed. If I was going to die here, no one was going to watch. I took a careful step into the room and off to the side, the door closing automatically behind me. The wolf watched me, ready to attack if I moved in a way it didn't like.

The only thing in the cell is a bed. I stepped behind it, putting my hands slowly on the footboard, and pushed. The wolf growled at the sound of the metal frame against the stone floor. I stopped, pointing to the camera. I hoped this wolf understood me and would be an ally when it finally shifted back to human — if I am still alive myself.

The wolf followed my hand to the camera. Its lips drew back as it attacked the camera knocking it out of the corner. The camera hung limply by its wires. The wolf now spun to face me. It lunged. I cursed, dodging to the side, but the wolf only landed on the bed. Then it quickly rebounded off it to push me down to the ground.

Fear flooded me as I fell face-first onto the stone floor. The wolf's paw on my back stopped me from crawling away. It then flipped me, its muzzle burying in my stomach and pushing up my shirt. I tried to stop the wolf by pushing its head down and away. It growled at me. My heart pounded loudly in my ears, and my throat was dry. I didn't think I could scream if it decided I was a threat and sunk its teeth into me.

The wolf sniffed me again and then made what I assumed was a sneezing noise. It then lay on the ground, its head resting on my stomach. I didn't know what to think. The wolf went from viciously trying to take down the door to a subdued wolf. The wolf closed its eyes. I tried to push out from under him, but the slightest movement had it growling at me again. I didn't dare make any other movements, afraid that it might consider me a threat after all and attack me instead of falling asleep as it did.

I inwardly cursed. I was stuck with my bruised back pressed firmly onto the stone floor until the wolf returned to its human form.

# Chapter Thirteen

## Ryan

MY MUSCLES GRUMBLED THEIR complaint from the shift I experienced last night. I never could get used to how sore they are after being a wolf all night long. A few hours I can handle, no problem. Wrapping my arms around my pillow, I pulled it with me as I shifted to my back. I didn't want to wake up.

The scent of candy apples wrapped around me, causing my stomach to growl. My mind — still half asleep — created the image of a giant candy apple in my arms. I began licking the candy, and I could swear the flavour coated my tongue. A gasp, or maybe it was a shriek, had me pausing mid-lick. Candy apples are not supposed to make noise. Pressure at my shoulders had me opening my eyes. My arms fell from what I thought was a pillow but was actually a human. That human pushed away, and large brown eyes stared down at me.

"Alice?" I wasn't sure if I was still dreaming.

"Ryan." The relief in her voice was palpable as she leaned back in, her hands on either side of my face and kissed me.

I wrapped my arms back around her, not wanting to let go. A whimper escaped her. I pushed her back, concerned I had injured her while I was a wolf. Then I wondered why she was even with me. I don't remember her being with me when I woke in this cell last night before I shifted into a wolf. The tranquillizer had lowered my control over my wolf, forcing the shift. ·

"Are you okay? Did I hurt you? Why are you here?"

"Ryan, slow down." She put a hand on my mouth to silence any further questions as she sat straddled on my chest. "You didn't hurt me. Alex Kingsley had me tossed in here."

"Why would he throw you into a room with a wolf?" I pulled her hand away.

"He was probably hoping I'd change my mind on his offer. Probably thought I'd do anything to survive, to get away from a furious wolf."

"What offer?" I growled out.

"We can cross reference our notes a little later." She waved me off. "First, we need to get out of here, find Bret and free my parents."

Worry filled me. "Bret is here?"

"I don't know. He was with me when I was taken, but we were shot with tranquillizers. When I came to, I was with my mother."

While she spoke, I stood up, placing her on the metal framed bed, and went to the door. I will get her out of here without any further injuries. I could feel her eyes on me as I worked at our escape.

"While I work on this, tell me what you know."

"Eventually, my father was brought to the room bloodied and bruised while I was taken to see the Kingsley's — Lucas and his father, Alex. Alex wants me to marry his son so they can get back into the Hunter Society and bring about changes. The vampire is working with them. I'm pretty sure he has other plans, but I'm not sure what they are yet."

Alice continued to talk. I tugged at the door; it didn't budge. I examined the hinges. Heavy duty but with the right tool, I might be able to free the door from the hinges. I looked around the room. The only thing in the cement block of a cell was the bed. Alice hopped off the bed as I pulled a leg off the metal frame. Placing the edge of the metal underneath the pin head, I used as much force as I dared to push it up.

"Here." Alice offered me her boot. "Use the heel like a hammer."

"When we get out of here, I'm taking you out for dinner." I told her, hoping to lighten the mood of our dire situation.

"Ryan." She said my name softly as if she were going to turn me down — again.

"When I read that SOS text from you, I panicked. I immediately went to your house." The first pin was out, and I started on the second one. "My heart dropped when I pulled up — the fire had engulfed the house though it was nearly out by the time I arrived."

"Fire?"

"I had your phone traced just to make sure you didn't go down with the house." I took in a ragged breath before moving on to the final pin. "Your phone was traced to the Kingsley's house."

The pin came out faster than the others — my anger over the look-a-like fueling my strike. I couldn't bring myself to tell Alice about the woman. I turned, handing her boot back. She mumbled a thank you as she put it back on. Seeing that look-a-like with Lucas hit me hard. For a millisecond, I thought I'd lost Alice to someone else. I knew it'd happen eventually, but seeing it had me regretting not pursuing her harder. I want Alice. I don't want her with anyone else, even if she deserves better than a monster like me.

I opened my mouth to tell her how I feel. She was looking at me with a hopeful look. I couldn't do it. Not now. Closing my mouth, I spun around, pulling the door away to reveal another door. This one, I noted, has a keypad next to it. One punch to fry the system, and I heard the lock disengaging. I waited a heartbeat to see if anyone was coming. No one. I couldn't even hear faint murmuring to indicate that anyone was around. The scent of blood though — overwhelming.

"Come on." I glanced over my shoulder to Alice. She held out a bed sheet to me. "What's that for?"

"To cover yourself up." She answered, a blush tainting her cheeks.

I looked down. Used to waking up after a shift in the nude, I didn't think twice about it. Taking it from her, I wrapped it around my lower half. Pushing the door open, Alice followed me out into the empty hall. I have no idea where to go.

Alice pointed to the left. "That is the way I came from."

"Let's go this way." I pointed to the right. "Just a little while to see if we can find Bret."

She looked hesitant, glancing back to the left, where I assumed her parents were, but she nodded reluctantly anyway. I didn't bother with being cautious. There are no sounds or other scents to tell me that we would come across someone else, only the scent of blood. After maybe five minutes, it was hard to tell with no means of time with us, the scent of blood became more potent than before. I halted suddenly. Alice bumped into my back.

"What is it?" She whispered, a soft hand on my back as she peered around me.

"I smell something." My answer was a low growl as I took in a better sniff of the air. "Bret."

"Which way?"

I didn't answer. I rushed off, following my nose. The heavy clicking of Alice's boots signalled that she followed me. I stopped in front of an open door, horror filling me. Alice stopped beside me, her hand clasped over her mouth with a gasp. Four bodies hung upside down, their blood pouring slowly into buckets below. One of those bodies belongs to Bret. Another wolf hung beside him, and two humans were on the far side of them.

"Oh my God, Bret!"

Alice rushed into the room before I could stop her. There could have been a trap or a warning system set up inside. Halting in front of him, she looked him over.

"We have to get him down." She glanced over at the others. "We have to get them all down."

I looked at how Bret was being hung. His ankles are chained to a rig in the ceiling, its wiring running along the length of the ceiling to a mechanism on the far wall.

"Hold his head." I ordered.

Alice did as she was told. I pushed the down button on the mechanism. It whirled to life, making a racket that anyone would have heard. Bret's body slowly lowered to the ground. Alice gently pushed the blood bucket aside with her foot to lower herself with him. I immediately un-did Bret's chained ankles and then checked for a pulse.

"Faint." The word came out in a relieved breath. Then, gently tapping Bret's cheek, I tried to get a reaction. "Come on, partner."

Bret grunted. It wasn't much, but it was something. I won't let my Beta die this way — or even in this place. I hauled him over my shoulders in a fireman's carry. The three of us are getting out of this place.

"What about the others?" Alice scrambled up. "I'm not leaving them hanging there."

I didn't want to waste my time on them, especially on the humans. "Check for a pulse."

Alice went to the farthest human, checking the neck. Her expression grim, she shook her head, looking at me pleadingly. I couldn't ignore that look. I put Bret down, then moved to the mechanism and together we lowered the two humans, who had no pulse, along with the wolf, whose pulse was faint. Alice looked around the room for a way to bring the other wolf. I picked Bret back up.

Bret stirred on my shoulders. "Ryan?"

"Hold on, partner."

Alice found a wheelchair hidden in a dark corner. I placed Bret in the chair and tossed the other wolf over my shoulders. The two of us hurried back the way we came. Our exit was blocked by another door with a keypad beside it. With the wolf over my shoulder in a fireman's carry, I couldn't punch it like I did to get out of the cell. Alice stepped up, pushing the wheelchair in front of me so it didn't roll away, then kicked at the keypad. Her heel getting stuck, I bit back a grin as she hopped on one foot, trying to free herself. She regained her foot as the doors opened.

The other side was clear of people and sound. The sudden brightness of the white hall blinded me. I blinked rapidly, readjusting to the new scenery. This time Alice led the way. I could hear her counting the doors we passed under her breath. Before continuing, she hesitated briefly at an open room with warm colours, oversized chairs, and a TV. I didn't ask her about it, her scowl telling me that's where she learnt about the Kingsley's being behind this mess.

The faintest scent of gunpowder and blood had me stopping at a hallway. "This way."

"But —." Alice looked down the hall she wanted to continue in. "My parents."

"Let's get you, Bret, and this wolf into the elevator that got me here. I'll backtrack to find your parents." I wanted to throw her over my shoulder and toss her into the elevator that I know is at the end of the hall when she didn't move. "The sooner you can call an ambulance, the sooner Bret will be treated."

"You promise to look for my parents?"

"Yes."

A gargled sound from Bret had her moving. The hall was long, and no guards protected the elevator this time. I got Alice, Bret, and the wolf inside, waiting for the doors to close before backtracking. I closed my eyes, focusing on the scent of roses and coffee that belonged to Alice's parents and followed it. Alice's faint scent from being with them helped my search. Finally, I stopped in front of the door, where their scents seemed to permeate. I tested the handle and slowly pushed the door open, tensing when another smell hit me.

"Now, this is a surprise."

I stared at the vampire in the room. His blond hair and blue eyes matched Alice's description after her attack. His scent is recognizable from all the crime scenes I've been to lately. He grinned at me, showing off his fangs. My hands clenched at my sides. The desire to rip those fangs out is overwhelming.

"I was hoping my Alice would come to me."

"She's not yours."

"And yet she came to find me the other night."

I clenched my hands at my side. "Where are her parents?"

He spread his hands out. "Not here."

"Where are they?"

"How about a trade?" The vampire's grin widened. "I'll tell you where the parents are if you hand over Alice."

I ground my teeth. Why does he want my Hunter so badly? I'll never let him have Alice. My priority right now is to get her parents back. This vampire is the only one with all the answers. The vampire watched me patiently, his grin fading into a relaxed smile. I hated that look on him.

"How about you tell me where they are, and I won't kill you."

The vampire laughed. "You can't kill me, Alpha."

"We'll see about that."

I lunged at the vampire, who dodged beneath me, countering with an uppercut, then quickly with a jab to my gut. I flew back with the force of his punch. The door at my back stopped me from going any further. Its soft metal formed around me from the impact. The vampire stood straighter, gently tugging at the cuffs of his shirt like he didn't just send me across the room. I wasn't going to be able to fight him in human form. With a growl, I began to shift, my wolf wanting a piece of this action. The shift from human to wolf came too slowly. It was too soon after my last change. But, of course, the vampire wouldn't let me finish.

A silver blade pierced my gut, its point dangerously close to my heart. The vampire was faster than Queen, faster than any other vampire I'd ever encountered. Stronger too. His power flowed over me, knocking the air out of me. It was so strong. My partial shift reverted to human.

"I want you alive, Alpha, long enough to see Alice come to me willingly. She'll be a queen in the empire I'm building."

# Chapter Fourteen

## Alice

The elevator doors opened. I pushed the wheelchair forward and dragged the other man Ryan placed in the elevator out by the wrists. I wanted to rush back into the elevator while my adrenaline was still high and help Ryan save my parents. But instead, the sudden sound of footsteps had me wishing I had a weapon as I spun to see who approached. I realized then that an officer was nearby, his hand resting on the radio attached to his shoulder.

"Miss Thorpe!" My eyes darted to Captain Forest's shocked face behind the officer. "Michaelson!"

"He's lost a lot of blood." I stated the obvious. "He needs a hospital."

"Get ambulances here!" The captain ordered the officer. "Miss Thorpe, what happened?"

"Ryan, he's still down there."

I gestured to the elevator behind me. Captain Forest spoke into a portable radio. More officers came from the hall behind him. He had them going down in three groups. I collapsed to my knees, a hand on Bret's knee. I felt useless. A Hunter should never be useless.

"Tell me what happened." Captain Forest knelt in front of me, his tone softer.

"Bret and I were kidnapped at the Richardson farm. When I came to, my mother was with me." I gave him a watered-down version of the events. "Guards brought my father, bloodied and bruised, to us, then took me away."

"Where did they take you?"

"To see my captor." I looked at him. "Alex and Lucas Kingsley."

Captain Forest stiffened. "Are you sure?"

"Yes."

"Why did they kidnap you?"

I looked away. The answer to that would reveal the supernatural world. Thankfully the paramedics arrived, and I was able to distract myself from the question. An officer came up the elevator, panicked and urged the paramedics down below. My heart sank. I stared at the elevator doors as they closed with the paramedics. Images of my father flooded my mind. Time seemed to slow as I waited for the paramedics to return.

The doors finally opened. The paramedics rushed out with a body on a gurney. Ryan lay there with a blade sticking out of him. I felt the world tilt, and I fell forward on my hands. I took in deep breaths. If Ryan was in this kind of condition, then what about my parents?

"Miss Thorpe." Hands clasped around my shoulders. "Miss Thorpe. I need a paramedic over here!"

"No!" I choked out. I didn't need medical attention. "I'm fine."

"You are not fine." Captain Forest told me sternly. "You need to be checked out."

I pushed myself to a seated position. I needed to refocus my thoughts. First, I needed to find my parents. Then, I needed to track down Carden. There is no way a Kingsley could have harmed Ryan that badly. So, it had to be Carden. It's the only logical explanation.

"What hospital are they going to?"

"Stellacote Hospital."

I pushed myself up to my feet. I have to keep my head on straight. "I need to make a phone call."

Captain Forest gave me the most confused and taken-back look I've ever seen. "Who do you plan on calling?"

"Captain, I don't have time to answer your questions." I knew I was being harsh, but I had to hurry. He handed me his phone, and I dialled Josie's number. I've called it so many times that the number is memorized. "Josie, it's Alice."

"Are you okay? I heard your house burned down." Her voice was a mere whisper.

"I'll tell you later. Right now, I need Queen."

"She's not available." Which meant it must be daytime.

"Ryan's life is on the balance."

Captain Forest was watching me with interest. I could hear Josie moving on the other end. First, Queen Ana's irritated voice could be heard, then Josie telling her why she was woken up during the day before Queen's voice came onto the line.

"Queen, I'm requesting a favour."

"What kind of favour young Hunter?" The vampire's voice inquired sweetly, but there was still an edge of irritation behind it.

"Ryan and Bret are in critical condition and in transport to Stellacote Hospital."

"You want me to give permission to allow them to stay and heal."

"Please." I begged.

There was a pause as she considered the request. "Very well, young Hunter."

"Thank you."

"I will collect payment for this favour."

"Of course."

I handed the phone back to Captain Forest. "You know about her too?"

"Her?"

He lowered his voice. "The vampire leader."

I stared at him wide-eyed. "This is not the place. Take me to the hospital."

Captain Forest nodded, leading me out of the building. I was surprised to find that I was at Stellacote University. The area swarmed with officers, and an extra ambulance was on standby in case they found anyone else. I buckled myself into the captain's car, realization hitting me.

"My parents."

"Detective Lune was the only one found down there."

I knew that wasn't true. "There are two other men down there."

"My men will find them." The captain assured me. "How do you know the vampire leader?"

"I have my connections." I responded cautiously. "What do you know captain?"

"I know vampires roam the city. Detective Lune convinced the leader not to wipe my memory, claiming it would be easier to do his job on supernatural cases."

I let that sink in. Ryan didn't tell him about wolves or Hunters, so I was careful not to bring either up. However, I wasn't sure how to explain how I knew Queen without explaining Hunters. So I held off on any explanation for as long as possible.

"Miss Thorpe, are you going to tell me anything?"

"I'd rather not." I admitted with a sigh. "There are parts of that world I am not at liberty to speak about. However, I can say that I am thankful that you know about vampires. It is rare for a human to know about them and not be working for them."

"Do you work for them?"

"In a way."

We arrived at the hospital. Captain Forest's badge got us information; while Bret was in ICU, Ryan was in surgery. I paced outside the doors to surgery while my mind raced. What happened to the Kingsley's and the victims I heard screaming? Why did everyone suddenly vanish? If my parents weren't down there, then where are they? Every question brought more questions.

"Michaelson is going to be okay." Captain Forest had left me to check on his other detective. "They put him on an IV drip and are replacing his lost blood. How's Detective Lune?"

"Still in surgery."

Just then, a doctor came out of the surgery room, his eyes flickering from me to the captain. "The surgery went well. We were able to stop the bleeding, but there was a lot of damage to his body. So right now, we're putting him in recovery. We'll assess his situation in a few days when he's recovered some strength."

I wasn't worried. His supernatural abilities will help with that. "Can I see him?"

The doctor glanced at the captain before leading us through the hospital. Bret and Ryan shared a room in the ICU, each occupying a bed on either side. My heart stopped at the sight of them hooked up to machines that monitored their vitals. I went over to Ryan, pulled a chair closer, and took his hand.

"Fight." I whispered.

"Two werewolves in my hospital." A musical voice sighed dramatically. "I never thought I'd see the day."

I blinked, trying to make out the figure in the dark. "Queen Ana?"

"Young Hunter."

My eyes focussed on the beautiful redhead with pale skin, piercing bright green eyes, and a commanding presence. She sauntered into the room, gaze fixed on mine. Stellacote Hospital is vampire territory. The hospital can supply them with blood from blood banks. They can even take sanctuary in the hospital if need be against any attack. Usually, werewolves go to another hospital in the city, but Bret and Ryan were already en route here, so I had to get them permission fast.

"Are you here to collect on that favour?" I inquired.

"We shall see." Queen stopped at the foot of Ryan's bed, turning only her head to view him. "What happened to the Alpha?"

"Carden Galinnor."

The name slipped past my lips shocking us both. I had never been able to say his name before and never knew his last name until now. Queen's eyes were wide and fearful. My face, I was sure, reflected that of Queen's. It scared me how easily that name was said now.

"How do you know that name?"

"He told me his first name." My chin was held tightly by perfectly manicured fingers. "What are you doing?"

"You said you were bitten by a vampire, but the Alpha cleansed you. Did that vampire bite you again?"

"No."

"Are you sure young Hunter?"

I couldn't answer. There was a period of utter unknown when I was tranquillized. What about that dream I had while in the rose maze? He bit me then, but does that count?

"With a single bite, the poison in our fangs can kill you humans, which is why we tend to drain you. Or if we are careful, we can inject just enough poison to be able to enter your mind. The Alpha may have cleansed you, but all he did was reduce the strength of the poison." Queen clicked her tongue, pulling back. "A second bite strengthens the connection, allowing the ability to go both ways."

I gripped Ryan's hand tighter. "Are you telling me that Carden bit me a second time?"

"It is the only way you would know his full name young Hunter. You read it from his mind."

"How? I don't understand." My head spun, and my stomach twisted. This information was too much. I would have loved to learn the intricacies of vampires — before I became a victim to them. "Do you know this vampire?"

"With a third bite and an exchanging of blood, he will be able to change you." The red-headed beauty hugged herself, her voice lowering. "Just like he changed me."

Silence fell between us. Queen's eyes drifted to Ryan. I watched her. The vampire didn't look at him with disgust but instead pity, or maybe it was longing. I couldn't tell. Bret stirred with pain-filled grunts. I went to him, gently touching his arm and speaking reassuring words to pull him from whatever nightmare plagued him.

"Ryan and I found him hanging upside down." I explained, feeling Queen's eyes on my back. "They were draining him."

"I cannot stop him young Hunter. He is my maker. What I can do is ensure that our laws do not get in your way."

"Do you really believe I can stop him alone?" I walked to the foot of Bret's bed. "Look what he did to the Alpha and Beta of Stellacote. I really am just a weak human."

"You are stronger than you know, my dear Hunter. Your father may have tolerated us supernatural for the sake of peace, but you have made friends of us. You must have more faith in yourself."

I stared up at Queen. "You called me Hunter."

"That is what you are."

"You've always called me young Hunter."

"Have I?" The faintest of smiles graced the vampire's lips. "I'd like to call upon that favour you owe me."

"Which is?"

"Do not let him turn you."

With that, Queen Ana left the hospital room. I stayed where I stood, looking over at Ryan. Physically I could not beat Carden. If he wanted me that badly I could always use that to get close to him and then kill him. First, I'd have to return home and hope the weapons room has remained intact. With a kiss on Ryan's cheek, I left the hospital.

# Chapter Fifteen

## Ryan

THAT BLUE-EYED VAMPIRE'S SMILE haunted me. My mind conjured up a very vivid nightmare of Alice being held in his arms while I was being bound, unable to do anything to keep them apart. When Alice went to him this time, she pulled her brown hair off her neck, allowing him to bite her. Her mouth opened in an 'O' shape, no sound escaping as she held him tighter. The nightmare jolted me awake. I looked around the room, trying to orient myself. I was hoping to find Alice but instead found my partner on the other side of the room looking at me, concerned. He had started to get out of bed when I woke.

"What happened? Where are we?"

"I don't know what happened, but it looks like we're in a hospital." Bret admitted, slipping on a pair of sweatpants that were folded onto a chair next to his bed. "Last thing I remember is Miss Thorpe and I were at the Richardson farm."

"Alice!" My eyes widened, the nightmare forefront of my mind. "Where's Alice?"

Bret frowned. "She wasn't here when I woke up."

"That vampire must have gotten to her."

Machines beside me started beeping wildly. Nurses came into the room, trying to get me to calm down and regulate the beeping. Too concerned for Alice, I kept pushing them away and pulling out the needles in my arms. Irritated, the nurses snapped at me urgently, expressing their worry that I needed to calm down and let them do their job of helping me recover. Eventually, one of them left the room in a panic.

A few minutes later, I recognized the director of Stellacote Hospital come into the room. "Let him be. If he wants to leave, let him leave."

The nurses looked at him like he was crazy but backed away and out of the room. He was one of Queen's humans. This meant Bret and I were in her territory and needed to leave. Immediately. I need to go to find Alice anyway. Captain Forest came in just as the last nurse left the room.

"Detectives." He let out a relieved sigh. "I'm so glad to see the two of you finally awake. It's been two days. I was beginning to worry."

The director eyed him, lips thinning. I swung my legs over the bed. I suspected the director wanted to tell me something but didn't want to in front of a human. Hobbling over to the end of the bed, I held onto the footboard and stared him down.

"He knows about her." I said.

The director flashed an irritated look my way but nodded and closed the door to the private room before speaking. "Queen wanted you to have this." He pulled out a small vile of red liquid. "She said you're going to need it when you woke up."

"What do you know?"

"I was told to hand this to you when you woke. She informed me that you'd know what to do."

Hugh's eyes widened, his mouth dropping open. "You know the vampire leader too? How many other people in this city know about vampires?"

"What do you mean?" Bret inquired, handing me another pair of sweatpants found in the room.

"Miss Thorpe also knows about the leader. From the one-sided conversation I heard, she asked for a favour to have you two stay here."

The director scowled, and I growled. Bret shook his head with a little sigh. The only one who didn't understand the meaning was the captain himself. The man looked between us, completely confused over the various reactions. Owing Queen Ana a favour could be dangerous. She could hold onto that favour for the rest of her life — which is a very long time — or it could be a favour so dangerous that it's the last thing you'd ever do.

"I need to find Alice."

"I'm surprised Miss Thorpe isn't here." Hugh pondered, staring past me to the chair by my bed. "She stayed the night on your first night here. I thought she'd never leave your side. Although, now that I think about it, I didn't see her yesterday."

"I need to find her." I repeated.

The director left the room. The conversation was not important to him. Bret swung my arm around his neck, helping me out of the room. He should be in worse condition, having his blood drained slowly. He should be the one needing help to walk, not me. Hugh followed us out of the hospital, detailing what he could of the events from when Alice surfaced at Stellacote University two days ago.

They are still in search of the Kingsley's along with the Thorpe's. I noted that Alice didn't tell him everything that happened beneath the university or what we are. Neither Bret nor I had a car, so Hugh drove us to my flat, where I could get my clothes. I was thankful that Hugh said he was returning to the station to send extra cops out to look for Alice. Manpower must be running low.

"Where are we starting?" Bret called out from the kitchen as I got changed.

"Call the pack. Have them start looking for Alice and have someone drop us off a car." I returned to the kitchen, taking a slice of the cold pizza Bret had pulled from my fridge. "We will be starting in Capital Hill."

Bret nodded. Picking up the receiver, he began the calls. Only three were needed. One was to get us a car, and the other two were to pack members who would pass the message along that Alice needed to be found. I pulled out the vial the director gave me and held it to the light. It contains Queen's blood, something I've had once before. It gave me fantastic speed, strength, and healing capabilities. The drawback is that it doesn't last very long and can deal quite a bit of damage to my body once it wears off. Werewolf and vampire blood should never mix. My first and last time drinking Queen's blood was when I became Alpha of Stellacote, and she needed my help to take down a vampire who was experimenting on himself to add and maintain the abilities of a werewolf to his DNA. I'll take it as a last resort, and only when I'm closer to this vampire. I stuffed the vile back into my pocket.

"Ten minutes until we get a car." Bret hung up the phone. "And our pack knows to search for Alice but to be careful of the vampire."

I grimaced. "Should have told them to be careful of the Kingsley's too. They were behind the kidnappings."

"Captain Forrest mentioned something about searching for them. Did you learn about the Kingsley's while with Roman?"

I explained what I had learnt while with the other Alpha as Bret borrowed some clothes. By the time the explanation was done, we were both caught up on everything that had been happening the car arrived. The pack member that dropped it off handed the keys over and was told to aid in the search for Alice. Something told me they wouldn't find her, but I had to try. I drove to the Thorpe house. It looked worse now that all the flames were gone and no more emergency crews were around. I remembered Alice stepping behind a grandfather clock the last time I was here. Jeffery had told Alice to grab weapons before we went to see Queen that night.

"What are we doing here?" Bret questioned.

"We're going to need weapons to go after the vampire."

"A pack member could have brought us some."

I shook my head. The Hunter weapons would be better than what I have stored in the house. Besides, the Thorpe house is much closer. It would have taken too long to gather the weapons from the house. The stairs leading upstairs were far too damaged for us to take. I walked underneath where the study was, a pile of concrete and stone at my feet. It looked like the area was disturbed but not thoroughly cleaned. With Bret's help, we cleared the pile to find the stairs I hoped to find. The two of us stepped into the darkness with me in the lead. The underground room appeared untouched by the damage above. Two tables were filled with all sorts of weapons.

"Gear up." I ordered, reaching for a gun and inspecting it before slipping it into the back of my jeans. "Besides the vampire, I don't know what else we're going to face."

Bret didn't say anything as he strapped on various guns. Bret was turned while on the battlefield. Before that, he was a sniper in the military. I found him and helped him through the first change. Unfortunately, a traitor used the opportunity to tell Bret's wife and daughter that he was dead and then took advantage of their grief. By the time he was in control enough of his wolf to return to them, it was too late. Bret went rogue, hunting down the traitor. I got to him just in time to stop him from doing something he would later regret.

I glanced at Bret. He wore the same expression he had all those years ago. "We will get Alice back."

"I know, but in what condition?"

I frowned. "Alice is not your daughter. Alice is a fighter; whatever that vampire does to her, we will dish out in greater amounts to him."

Bret smiled faintly. "Let's get our Hunter back."

"First, let's go to the Kingsley's house and see what information they left behind."

"Do you think they'd be stupid enough to leave evidence behind?"

"They are on the run. Hugh said they haven't been able to find them." I pointed out. "It's worth a shot. Besides, he wouldn't know what to look for. We do."

With guns and blades strapped on, Bret and I are ready to take out a small army. I took a quick look around the hidden room. It is the perfect training room. Despite all of Alice's training, this vampire is still out of her league. Out of mine too. I will do everything I can for Alice to end this vampire's life, including taking Queen's blood and giving in to the monster within.

I parked at the very end of the Kingsley's driveway. It will slow down anyone trying to escape, but if anyone is in the house, they won't see us coming. With guns in hand, we took up either side of the wide driveway, senses trained to every little sound. Unfortunately, the soft chirp of birds and the gentle breeze rustling the leaves were all that could be heard. No footsteps, mumbled voices, or even the whisper of someone breathing. This did not bode well for finding Alice or the Kingsley's.

The front door was left unlocked. Ominous. Or maybe just lucky. We cleared the main floor, then the upstairs. On our way back down, we were met by Alice. She waited for us at the bottom of the stairs. She looked up at us with a glazed expression. The vampire had taken complete control of her mind.

"I've been waiting for you." Alice smiled coolly.

"Alice, you need to fight the vampire's control." I called down to her. "He's using you."

"My king would never do that. I am his queen."

She raised a gun and shot at us, forcing us back into the upstairs hall, where there was a wall to block the bullets. Bret and I exchanged looks. We couldn't harm Alice. Not severely anyway. With all her training, she'd be a formidable opponent to disarm and bind. We need a strategy and fast.

"This isn't going to be easy." Bret stated.

"We need to trap her." I whispered. Her footsteps could be heard slowly coming up the stairs. "Then we need to break the vampire's control on her."

"First, we need to free her of that gun. Miss Thorpe shouldn't be as dangerous without a weapon."

"Have you ever seen her with a gun before?"

Bret furrowed his brows at that question, pondering. I've only seen her use a sword. My partner shook his head.

"If we're lucky, she can't aim well." He answered finally.

Alice made her way to the top of the stairs. A bullet landed in the wall above my head. I frowned, hoping that was just her lousy aim, not a warning shot. I shot at her feet, stopping her advance and giving us a chance to move further down the hall. Bret pointed out a smaller guest bedroom that we had cleared earlier. I stayed outside the room to ensure that Alice followed us before ducking inside. Hiding behind the door, my heart pounded as I listened to her careful steps toward us. She hesitated just beyond the door. Then, finally, she stepped in.

Bret slammed the door shut, and I tackled Alice as she turned to us. The gun in her hand went skittering across the floor. She jabbed her elbow down on the back of my neck. I growled. She squirmed until she had rolled us, our positions alternating. I kept a tight grip on her. Alice kneed me. My grip loosened. She jumped back. Forgetting about Bret in the room, my Beta knocked her out with the butt of his gun to the back of her neck.

"Thanks." My voice came out gruff as I rolled to my feet. "Let's get her tied up."

Bret took sheets from the bed, wrapping them around Alice's arms and legs, preventing her from lashing out when she came to. I couldn't wait for her to wake up naturally. Carrying her to the bathroom, I placed her in the tub and turned on the cold water. Alice jolted awake, cursing about the water being cold. I turned it off, thankful that the glazed expression was gone when she glared up at me. However, that didn't mean the vampire was out of her mind.

## Chapter Sixteen

### Alice

COLD WATER PIERCED THROUGH my clothes. My reaction was to jump away from the drastic temperature change, but I found myself bound and stuck in a tub. I glared first at the water and then at whoever had turned it on. A man with brown hair and brown eyes looked down at me, but I just continued to glare. His looks tickled the back of my mind, but I didn't pay them any attention.

"Don't give me that look." He growled, turning the water off.

"What's with the cold shower?"

"Miss Thorpe, is the vampire here?" Another voice drew my attention, and I looked to see another man with glasses.

"Vampire?" I questioned, my voice sounding distant even to my ears. Blue eyes seared across my memory. "What vampire?"

"The one that bit you." The brown-eyed man struggled to control the anger in his voice.

"Oh, you mean Carden. My king's not here." I didn't miss the look exchanged between the two men. "Did you need him for something?"

"Yes." Glasses answered, placing a hand on the other's shoulder. "We just wanted to ask him about your parents."

My eyes fell onto the weapons they carried. "Is that all?"

"We came prepared in case negotiations went sideways."

"Negotiations won't be necessary."

"Why is that?"

"Carden doesn't want my parents."

"What does he want Miss Thorpe?"

I looked at him, smiling. "Me, of course."

"He won't have you!" The brown-eyed man exclaimed, a low growl emphasizing his point. "I won't let him."

"But I'm already his queen."

"No, you're mine."

I watched his eyes fill with murderous intent.

"I'm not letting anyone have you."

"Ryan!" Glasses scolded. "Let me have a moment with Miss Thorpe."

The one named Ryan scowled, leaving the bathroom and slamming the door shut on his way out in frustration. The other one sat on the tile floor next to the tub. I watched him. His movements were careful, and he was surprisingly calm. What irritated me the most was that he didn't say anything.

"What?"

"Miss Thorpe, I want you to close your eyes for me."

"Why?"

A faint smile touched his lips. "Amuse me."

"Fine." I closed my eyes. "Happy now?"

"Tell me what you see."

I hesitated. "Blue eyes."

"Do you hear a voice?"

I nodded.

"What does it say?"

"Don't trust them." I told him.

"Now, I want you to picture your parents, Patty, or Ryan." He continued.

My brows knitted together with the effort. Nothing came to mind. I should know what my parents look like, shouldn't I? And Ryan, I just saw him, yet I can't seem to conjure up an image of him in my mind.

"What about Queen?"

I sucked in a breath. "I can't. Why can't I remember what my parents look like?"

"The vampire, the one you call Carden, has a hold on you. Those eyes you see are his. I need you to fight his control and come back to us."

I felt my head pound with the effort. The blue eyes I saw behind closed lids kept my focus, and they seemed to glow brighter when I tried to remember anything beyond those eyes. There should be more beyond those eyes. I felt him fighting me as I tried to regain control, fighting to keep me, but I didn't want to stay with him. He felt wrong, Carden felt wrong, and he made me feel cold.

Warm hands clasped my face forcing me to tilt my head upward. I kept my eyes shut. A scream escaped me from not only the contrast of temperatures running through me but from the vampire. Carden's power flowed through me more strongly than before. My vision was becoming almost blinded by how bright his blue eyes were becoming behind my closed lids.

Warm lips pressed onto mine. The blue eyes wavered as warmth filled me. I leaned into the heat. The blue eyes faded, being replaced by familiar brown eyes. My memory placed those brown eyes with Ryan, then I remembered Patty and how I had last seen my parents. A gasp escaped me. I opened my eyes.

Ryan looked at me, my face still in his hands. "Alice?"

"The hospital let you go?"

"You don't remember shooting at us or even talking to us just moments ago?" His brow furred.

"I shot at you?" I looked down at myself. "Why am I bound and in a bathtub? What happened to me?"

Relief filled Ryan's features. "The vampire took control of you. You were shooting at us when we came here looking for clues or even the Kingsley's themselves. But, instead, we found you."

"I don't use guns. I prefer to have a blade in my hands."

"Now that you're back with us." He helped to remove the bindings around me. "We can go find that vampire. He added another reason on the long list of why I want to tear him limb from limb."

I couldn't help myself. I laughed. Stepping out of the tub, I rolled my neck and shoulders. This vampire is never going to leave Stellacote. Not only did he bite me twice and control me, he still has my parents — at least, I believe he does. Bret offered me the sword he wore around his waist. I took it with a grateful nod.

Ryan took my hand in his. All three of us left the bathroom and went to the stairs. That's when he let go of me, filling his hand with a gun instead. Bret took the lead with Ryan close behind, and I saw their police training taking precedence. With my hand on the sword, I had it partially drawn, ready to block or defend when needed and followed them.

They went straight for the basement door, not even bothering to clear the main floor. The lights stayed off as we walked down the stairs. I walked a little slower. My vision was not as good in the dark as the supernatural. Ryan stopped me at the foot of the steps in a silent order not to move as he and Bret searched the basement. Bret returned to fetch me, leading me around the stairs to where Ryan waited at an open door.

I peered through the door. From what I could tell, the hall beyond was dimly lit and very long and not very wide either. A rancid smell came from within. Bret again took the lead. The further we walked, the more potent the awful smell became. Mumbled voices could be heard from the end of the hall.

Ryan stopped, a hand shooting out to tuck me behind him. The path we walked split into two hallways, while just ahead was an open doorway. Ryan guided me to the right of the open entrance, our bodies pressed as firmly as possible to the hallway walls to not be seen through the door. Bret, I saw, took up the left. They kept looking through the doorway. I wanted to see what they saw, but Ryan wouldn't let me move from my spot. I gripped my sword as I felt Carden speak into my head. I leaned into Ryan, hoping his warmth and presence alone could stop the voice and those eyes from controlling me again.

"He knows." I whispered tensely.

Ryan stiffened. Taking a vile from his pocket, he drank it before moving through the doorway into a wide-open area made entirely of stone. Carden sat on a throne-like chair, his legs stretched out and ankles crossed. Surrounding him — and us — are vampires, so many vampires with their fangs bared. I recognized a couple of Sanguis within the sea of vampires.

"Alpha, it's so good to see you again." I peered around Ryan to see Carden smiling. "And you brought Alice back to me."

"I've already told you that she's not yours."

"Why do you want her so badly?" Bret interjected.

"With Alice as my queen, I will return us to our glory days." Carden smiled.

The group he'd formed all cheered in response. Ryan hunched forward, his muscles rippling. He was shifting. I stepped away from him, not wanting to get in the way of his shift.

I looked at Carden. "Where are my parents?"

Carden stood gracefully, his arms gesturing to the space around him. "They aren't here. Come to me Alice."

I felt a pull toward him, Queen's favour ringing softly in my head. Pushing away from Ryan, I dug my heels into the ground and spoke clearly. "Carden Gallinor, by order of the Hunter Society, you shall not leave Stellacote."

"Oh?" He looked amused. "On what grounds do they have to forbid me from leaving this city?"

"You've murdered Hunters." Ryan added in a low growly voice. "And you've murdered innocent humans. As a member of Stellacote police, you are under arrest, but if you choose to fight, we will put you down."

"No human police force will be able to hold me."

"Then please fight. I would love to put you down."

"I'm sure you would." Carden's eyes fell on me. "Do you want me to be put down, my dear Alice?"

The words ran across my skin in a cold chill. I walked toward him, stopping somewhere between him and Ryan. Ryan growled at me to stay away from him. I drew my sword. Carden frowned. One of his vampires handed him a sword.

"I don't want to fight you Alice."

"I owe a favour, and I don't plan on failing to fulfill it."

Carden came at me. I barely had time to block his under attack. My knees buckled at the strength of his attack. All I needed was an opportunity to use the weapon I took from the safe. Instead, Carden played with me, his attacks slow enough that I could block but too fast for me to counterattack, and they stayed strong. He was pushing me further away from Ryan.

Annoyance filled his face. "Enough Alice."

His speed picked up, and he kicked me in the stomach instead of attacking with his sword. I flew across the room, my bruised back hitting the high back of his throne. I slid down, collapsing into the throne seat, struggling to breathe. Carden slipped his hand behind my neck, twisting his fingers in my hair, lifting me and leaning into my neck.

"Get away from her!" Ryan growled at the same time I heard a gunshot.

Carden flinched. "Stay out of this Alpha!"

The vampires hanging around the room's edges swarmed Ryan and Bret. I heard the sound of gunshots and growls. I couldn't see what was happening. Everyone moved too fast. And Carden blocked most of my view.

"Now, where was I?" Carden leaned back in toward me.

I let him lean in. I even tilted my neck for him and brought a hand up between us. A pleased sound came from Carden. While he was distracted by my false acceptance of his bite. I pulled out the secret weapon from my bra — a needle holding liquid silver. Once the silver is in Carden, it will flow through his system quickly, burning him from the inside out. This unique batch of fast-spreading liquid silver has a Hunter Society twist. The silver will attach itself to whatever blood cells it can within the vampire's body and multiply.

His fangs brushed my neck. I heard Ryan cry out. An animalistic sound I've never heard before. Feeling the tips of his fangs on my skin, I jabbed the needle into his neck. He growled in annoyance, pulling the now empty needle out and throwing it away. I didn't want to be near him when he realized what was happening inside his body. I brought the sword up that I still held loosely in my hand, cut my hair from his grip, and then scrambled away.

Carden's eyes widened, a scream emanating from him that sounded almost demonic. He scratched at his chest as if trying to get to a bomb that was about to go off. He glared at me, a curse on his lips as I watched him burst into flame. Everyone watched the spot where Carden had been. The remaining vampires Bret and Ryan could not defeat scurried out of the room.

At that moment, I didn't care that they were running. Instead, I stared at the spot Carden once stood, utterly horrified at what I had just done. Slicing off his head was different. At least a body remained, but burning from the inside out made my stomach curdle.

I felt Ryan come up behind me. Turning, I looked at him. He was partly shifted. A monstrous sight. Ryan extended his arm, a single claw brushing my cheek. I stared into Ryan's eyes. They were still the same brown I was used to seeing. He let out a growl turning to leave me. I felt cold without him there. Bret replaced him, wrapped an arm around me and led me out of this place.

# EPILOGUE

## RYAN

THE AFTERMATH OF USING Queen's blood, combined with not being fully healed before going after the vampire, caused me to return to the hospital. Though Queen offered to let me return to Stellacote Hospital, I didn't want to owe her a favour for the supposedly kind gesture and went to the other hospital in the city instead. I spent two weeks in bed recuperating.

During that time, Hugh finally found the Kingsley's at a private airport, trying to escape the city with Jeffery and Vivian. They were sent to the hospital to be looked after. Alice, who had, to my surprise, spent the first few days with me, ran to her parents' side once she heard about their rescue. The Kingsley's were being charged with kidnapping. Unfortunately they couldn't connect the Capital Hill murders to them.

While I was temporarily out of commission, Bret took up his role as Beta. He gathered the pack, explaining what had happened and keeping them calm. He also finalized the paperwork for the Capital Hill Killer. He made up a story about the FBI swooping in and taking the killer away. It was the best we could do with nothing to show the public.

163

The only thing remaining was to find the other Hunters, who I was sure were still alive. After two weeks in the hospital, I searched every property Alex Kingsley owned in and around the city. I found the missing Hunters on a property two cities over with nothing around for miles. I made sure they all returned home safely before I returned to work.

Hugh had me undergo training again to ensure I was ready to be on duty. By the time I was cleared, it was nearly two months after the incident. I hadn't heard anything from Alice since she left my side, which worried me. I had tracked down her parents. They lived in a much smaller home closer to Stellacote's core. I stopped by for a visit.

"Ryan." Jeffery welcomed me into their new home when I found myself on their front porch. "How are you?"

I smiled faintly. "I should be asking you that."

"Nothing a veteran Hunter like myself can't heal from."

"That is good to hear. What about your wife?"

The man frowned. "She must visit a doctor daily to help her deal with the trauma. The mental problems she had before the events didn't help anything."

"How is Alice dealing with that?"

He shrugged. "I haven't seen much of her. The Hunter Society has been keeping her busy. From what I gather, she's working on changing their older ways so we don't get another Kingsley incident."

I deflated; I was hoping to see her. "That's good."

"Have you been able to speak to her?"

"No, I haven't. I was hoping she was home."

"She doesn't live here anymore." He answered surprised. "She's been staying at her apartment when she does return to the city after a Hunter-sanctioned mission. We try to maintain a routine of weekly family dinners. They seem to help her mother."

"I guess I'll be going now." I turned to leave, hand on the door handle, when I paused. "I wish I could have done more."

"You have done plenty." Jeffery patted my shoulder. "Now, go to my daughter and ask her to marry you before some other Hunter falls for her."

I stiffened, glancing back at the man. He was smiling, almost laughing. Then, reaching around me, he pulled the door open and pushed me onto the porch. I stood there staring at the door letting the words sink in. Jeffery is right, someone in the Hunter Society is bound to fall for Alice, and I won't let her slip away from me. To hell with our social status. To hell with our titles. I want Alice. That's all that should matter. With new determination, I booked it over to her apartment.

In front of her apartment door, I hesitated. I could smell her on the other side but couldn't bring myself to raise my hand and knock. I gave myself a mental pep all the way here, yet here I stood, frozen in place. A soft click told me that Alice had unlocked the door, but it didn't open. I took a deep breath and entered her apartment.

Her hair was still short. I thought she might grow her hair back out. I liked her hair long, but she looked just as beautiful with it short. I thought she looked different, not just the hair or the silver choker she now wore around her neck. It was like there was a barrier hiding her from the world. Her muscles were stiff, and her jaw was set. This isn't the same Alice I fell in love with. This Alice is stronger for what she's been through. More beautiful and more vulnerable.

She didn't look at me when I entered. She was in the kitchen, took a breath and picked up the knife I assumed she put down to unlock the door. I closed and locked the door. This might be harder than I anticipated.

"It's not wise to leave your door unlocked." I scolded teasingly, trying to lighten the mood within the small apartment.

Alice used the knife to point to her phone sitting on the counter. "I saw you standing there."

"Oh." I didn't even see the camera in the hall. "How have you been?"

"Fine." She shrugged. "When did you get out of the hospital?"

"After two weeks." I didn't understand why there was this barrier between us. "I missed you."

A flicker of whom Alice used to be flashed across her features. I moved from the entryway to stand on the opposite side of the counter. She pointedly didn't look at me now. I need her to look at me. I need to know that despite everything, the Alice in front of me is the same as the Alice before.

"I've been busy with Hunter stuff. I'm helping to change things."

"Alice." I said her name so softly that her entire body froze. "I'm glad you're okay."

"It's my fault."

She spoke so softly that if I didn't have the hearing of a wolf, I would have never heard her. "Nothing is your fault."

"You were hurt because of me."

I moved to the other side of the counter, spinning her and cupping her face forcing her to look at me. "Nothing is your fault."

"Ryan, you were hurt. My parents were hurt. I wasn't strong enough." Her hand tightened on the knife.

I now understood why she didn't look at me. She felt guilty. "Listen to me very carefully. Nothing is your fault. Alex Kingsley held a grudge against the Hunter Society. Alex Kingsley started this whole thing. That vampire prayed on his hatred and need for revenge, using it as an excuse to harm innocent humans. He would have killed the Kingsleys once they were no longer needed. I will repeat this as often as I need to: nothing is your fault."

"If I was stronger, I could have dealt with Carden when he first attacked me."

"Then I wouldn't have been able to rush to your rescue."

"If I knew more about Hunter politics, I could have figured things out sooner." Alice let go of the knife in favour of gripping my wrists. "I was useless. I put you and Bret and my parents in danger."

"I will always come to your rescue."

"Why?"

"Because I love you, Alice Marigold Thorpe." I kissed her softly. "And I never want to let you go."

She shook, eyes glistening with unshed tears. "You deserve someone better than me."

"That's what I kept telling myself." I chuckled dryly. "I don't want anyone else but you. I want to spend the rest of our lives together."

"Ryan."

"Will you marry me?"

A slow smile crept across Alice's features, revealing her old self. The barrier she had created crumbled instantly. She didn't say anything, only nodded. I kissed her again. More fiercely this time. I won't let her go or allow anyone else to have her. She is mine.

# ABOUT AUTHOR

Ivy Marie grew up an army brat. Moving every two or three years, and finally settling in Ottawa, Ontario, Canada. When she's not writing she's at work, or spending time with her friends.

Both friends and family are supportive of her creative expression. She's found comfort in Supernatural Romance, with werewolves and vampires as the main creatures she writes about, and also in Contemporary Romance.

Ivy Marie writes for her own enjoyment. She also hopes that the joy she feels while writing is expressed and passed on to you.

# CONNECT

**I really appreciate you reading my book! Here are my social media coordinates;**

Facebook: www.facebook.com/IvysStolenHearts

Instagram: ivymariebooks

Blue Sky: @ivymarie-author.bsky.social

X: @IvyMarie_Books

Website: www.ivymarieauthor.com

**Don't forget about my wonderful cover artist - Shawna Russ;**

Instagram: shawncolourart

# ALSO BY

**Keep an eye out other books by Ivy Marie.**

*Contemporary Romance*
Thief in Paris
Bad Decisions (Book 1 of Decisions Duet)
Late Decisions (Book 2 of Decisions Duet)
Surprised by Love ~ Coming 2025
Fan the Flames ~ Coming 2026

*Paranormal Romance*
Stolen Heart
His Hunter
Bound to the Reaper (Book 1 of Reaper)
Reaper Undercover (Book 2 of Reaper) ~ Coming 2026
Reaper Forever (Book 3 of Reaper) ~ Coming 2027
Witch Troubles ~ Coming 2025

*Like Hell series (Paranormal Romance)* ~ Coming 2028

IVY MARIE

Like Hell Mario (Prequel)

Like Hell this is Real (Book 1)

Like Hell this is Normal (Book 2)

Like Hell this is Happening (Book 3)

Like Hell Alternative (Alternate Reality)